Mr. Down for Whatever

BAES OF JUNETEENTH

ELLE WRIGHT

This is a work of fiction. Any references to historical events, real people, or real places are used fictitiously. Other names, characters, places, and events are products of the author's imagination, and any resemblance to actual events or places or persons, living or dead, is entirely coincidental.

Mr. Down for Whatever

Paperback ISBN: 979-8-9854542-4-6

Elle Wrights Books, LLC
Ypsilanti, Michigan
www.ElleWright.com

Copy Editor/Proofreading:
Melissa Ringsted
There For You Editing

Cover Design:
Sherelle Green

Mr. Down for Whatever

Have you ever received the wrong text from the right person?

One thing about me? I don't play games. Another thing about me? I don't waste time.

I've built my reputation by treating my patients, my students, and my colleagues with respect.

In my role as Mr. Black Detroit, my focus is supporting my community and planning the city's annual Juneteenth celebration.

Again, my time is valuable. I should've ignored the text. But… There's something about Daphne that makes me want to engage. Maybe it's the way she commands a room and isn't afraid to get her hands dirty. Or maybe it's the glimpse of vulnerability in her eyes. It's probably just her. Whatever it is in the beginning quickly morphs into something else entirely, though.

Soon, I can't get enough of her. But can I convince her to take a chance on me?

Dear Reader

Heyyyy!!!!

It's been such an honor to work on this series!

I've written three Bae stories, and this one was so different for me. For one, the hero and the heroine are in their forties! Grown. And Sexy! Then, bringing Juneteenth into it … I enjoyed writing about how impactful this holiday is to so many people. I especially loved writing about Detroit!

Nero is one of those heroes I want to bottle up and keep for a rainy day. I loved his journey to forever with Daphne.

I hope you enjoy them!

Love,

Elle

www.ellewright.com

For everyone who died in and for the struggle.

MR. BLACK ORGANIZATION

Every legacy has a story … this is ours.

NERO

February, This Year

"A legacy forged in fire and created with a vision for our future."

My grandfather's words filtered through my mind as I stared at the African American Historical Museum before me. A cold chill crept up my spine. Despite the strides made, the triumphs shared, it almost felt like their efforts weren't enough. While I wouldn't discount progress, our communities were struggling to remain the vibrant beacons of light our elders fought so hard to build. Inspiration had yielded to influence. Social media had replaced face-to-face contact. Respect for each other seemed to be a thing of the past. "*We shall overcome*" became "*It's all about me.*" Our elders were dying. The bridge to the past was buckling under pressure.

I crept around the back of the museum. Before I arrived earlier, I'd studied the hand drawn map for hours, memorizing the distinct script on the tattered page. My grandfather's writing.

Levi Bond.

Better known as Ace.

I was here today because of him, because of the urgency in his spirit that had propelled him to link up with a group of powerful men to form a secret brotherhood. The mission was as clear then as it was now. To uplift. To protect. To restore. *By any means necessary.*

The groundskeepers had done a good job of maintaining the expansive lawn, making my trek easier. It took several minutes to get to my destination, just long enough for me to regret wearing a three-piece suit and a pair of Christian Louboutin shoes. But the directions on the map led me to an abandoned shack on the outskirts of the property, preserved through the community's efforts to designate this site a historical landmark. After glancing at my watch, I studied the structure. Traveling to this place served a dual purpose, and while I didn't mind getting my hands dirty, I had business to handle.

My phone buzzed in my pocket. I answered, "Yeah, Ace."

My grandfather's low voice came through the speaker. "Did you find it?"

"I'm here now. Still not sure why you encouraged me to dress up if I had to walk a muthafuckin' mile in these damn shoes." The suit I didn't mind. But these damn shoes? I learned the hard way on my first day as a resident, wandering the halls at the University of Michigan Medical Center, that comfortable shoes were a necessity for my job.

Ace laughed. "Sometimes you have to get dirty to find the treasure. Remember that."

I grumbled another curse. "Alright. I'll call you when I'm done with everything." I ended the call and made my way into the shack, using the trick my grandfather had shown me on the door. Luckily, his memory was impeccable because I was able to retrieve the case he'd stored there and make it back to the museum in record time.

Dusting myself off, I made the short walk to the entrance of the underground bunker, the place where it all started. Decades ago, five men formed the Mr. Black Organization under the cloak of secrecy. Today, the organization had chapters in every state and members in every sector of society from celebrities and professional athletes to clergymen and business moguls.

To honor my grandfather's commitment, I joined the organization at twenty-one and had remained a dues-paying member ever since. And while I respected the original mission of the organization, my career and my family had been my priority. Until now. As the current Mr. Black Detroit, I hoped to make impactful changes to my community and the organization during my time as the figurehead for our chapter.

As I neared the meeting space, I glanced at the pictures lining the walls in the hallway. I paused at a black and white image of Ace hanging on the wall, emerging from the shadows. *The way he lives his life.* The photograph was one I'd seen before many times, but seeing it there filled me with pride. I peered up the man who raised me and felt the weight of responsibility on my shoulders. Because I was the last Mr. Bond in his bloodline. Thankfully, Ace had brothers who had sons and grandsons, but Ace only had me. And I wouldn't let him down.

I was so engrossed in my thoughts that I hadn't realized Preston was standing next to me. I eyed him out of the corner of his eye. "What's up?" I murmured, forcing my attention back to the present.

Preston's gaze remained on my grandfather's portrait. "It's been a long time coming, huh?"

The fact that all five founding members of the organization had legacies serving in Mr. Black roles for their respective cities wasn't lost on me. Dante Powell. Preston Scott. Titan Stone. Porter Crowne. All of us tied by the bonds our grandfathers and great-grandfathers had made in this very room decades ago.

"From my perspective, we should take this as a sign," Preston continued. "It's time to take this organization back to its roots."

I observed the man next to me. Although Preston was younger than me, his serious demeanor reminded me of my grandfather. Intense. Intentional. Intelligent. We had that in common, so I was certain this meeting would be the start of something unforgettable. *And I'm down for whatever is necessary.*

"That's what I'm talking about, brotha." I held out a fist, and he bumped it with his.

I followed Preston into the room and greeted Titan with a dap. "What's good, man?"

"Same shit, different day," I grumbled, glancing back at Preston, who had his head buried in a book. "You good?"

Titan waved a dismissive hand. "Yeah. Guy had me cracking up before you got here."

"How's the family?" I asked. Distance had limited

interactions between the families, but we kept up with each other in various ways. Usually, off the grid. "It's been a minute."

While Titan and I caught up, Dante arrived and joined the conversation. Soon, the discussion veered into heated territory as we debated the current NBA season.

"I don't care what no one says, the Mavs should have taken it last year," Titan proudly proclaimed.

I waved a dismissive hand. "Man, please. Y'all Dallas fans have always been delusional."

"They're not the only ones. When Detroit makes the playoffs, maybe you can talk to me," Dante taunted. "Better yet, why don't you just give it up and root for the winning team?"

As usual, Detroit stayed losing, but I was a diehard Pistons fan. I could—*and would*—talk shit until the day I died. "That won't be L.A., so I'll gladly put my money on The Nuggets."

Dante grumbled a curse. "Whatever, man. We got this."

"In your dreams," I retorted.

Finally, Porter entered the room. Of all the gentlemen in the room, I'd interacted with Porter and his family the most since Chicago was a mere four-hour drive from Detroit.

"Nice of you to finally show the fuck up," Titan said, giving Porter a dap.

"You know me." While all of us commented on his penchant for being late, Porter made his way around the room before he stopped at me. "Good to see you, old man."

I chuckled. "Not too old to whoop yo' ass."

"How's your daughter?" he asked, a mischievous glint in his eyes. "Isn't she graduating from Michigan this year?"

My oldest daughter, Zoe, had followed in my footsteps and would graduate from University of Michigan Medical School this year. "Tread lightly, young brotha."

Cracking up, Porter patted my back. "I'm a man. And Zoe is beautiful."

"Beautiful and off-limits to you." It was all in fun. I knew Porter wasn't serious. Even if he was, it wasn't going to happen because Zoe had been living with her girlfriend for two years now. "Tell your father to get at me, though."

Preston cleared his throat, interrupting our conversation. "Okay, let's get started." He took out his tablet. "As part of the founding families, we've all been members of Mr. Black since we turned twenty-one. Yet, it wasn't until I was attending the networking event this past October that I realized for the first time since our grandfathers and great-grandfathers stood in this room, that each founding family has a member as the chosen Mr. Black rep for their city right now."

It had been over fifty years, which was a damn shame. The brothas on the wall in the hallway had paved the way for the organization to exist and had slowly been pushed out as the tumultuous civil rights era gave way to Reaganomics and the pursuit of the almighty dollar. Somewhere along the line, money became more important than justice. Now the erasure of our culture through various laws and political show threatened everything our forefathers had worked so hard to attain. The freedom to live.

"I suspected it had been a while," Titan said. "But I must have been so busy with work, I didn't realize this was the first time in over fifty years."

Preston nodded. "I don't think the National Executive Board realizes it either."

I thought back to something Ace had told me years

ago. "*You don't have to care to be affected.*" I recalled a moment me and Ace shared during one of the national meetings several years ago. When the conference opened with a popular rapper taking the stage and disrespecting Black women, Ace was disappointed. As if that wasn't bad enough, Mr. Black Boise had given an impassioned speech about our community's reliance on welfare checks and food stamps. He'd implored us to turn away from our past oppression because racism had been eradicated in America. The man even stated the reasons why Affirmative Action had harmed the race.

Before the speech ended, Ace asked me to follow him. We ended up at a neighborhood basketball court. As we watched the young men play the game, he shared a story about his childhood, about how hard he'd had to fight just to be able to play basketball in the open without harassment. I remembered the look in his eyes, the sadness, the disappointment. He'd placed his hand on my heart and encouraged me to step outside of the examination room and walk a mile in the community. That experience had changed my trajectory and my practice. Ultimately, it had propelled me to accept the nomination from the Detroit chapter and step into the role Ace had originated. So that I could make the change needed.

Dante agreed with Preston. "If they had, no doubt they would have called us into a private meeting at the event."

I tapped my fingers on the table. "And I still can't get over the fact that none of the members of our families are sitting on the board right now." But even as I said it, I knew that was by design. Many of my family members had been deemed too militant, too focused on the struggle.

Before I could call it out, Porter did. He was right. The executive board was full of shit. Since all of us were serving in critical roles within our own communities, we had a prime opportunity to do whatever the hell we needed to do. The conversation went on from there, with each of us voicing our concerns and pondering potential changes.

Preston cleared his throat. "I wanted you all here because Juneteenth is in less than four months, and I think we should make this the most impactful one yet. Change must happen now. Not tomorrow. Not with the next Mr. Black. Right now is our time, fellas, and we best use it effectively."

As we tossed out ideas, we all resolved to utilize our annual Juneteenth events to target the youth. With a focus on education, we would teach the young, Black men in our communities to aim high, to seek knowledge, to give back—whether it was through tech, history, community events, finance, or health.

Porter pulled out a fifth of imported whiskey and poured three shots for each of us. Tapping the first shot glass on the table, I took it for our grandfathers and great-grandfathers—to pay homage to their vision. The second shot was for my brother, Shaun, who lost his life far too soon. And the last shot ... Instead of pouring it on the floor, I tossed it back for the brothas who died *in* and *for* the struggle.

As we exchanged ideas, outlined our blueprint for action, I realized it was fate that brought us there tonight. Our forefathers had lit the match. Time and experience had prepared us for this mission. We were all at the same place, at the same time, for a reason. And despite what everyone else thought about decorum and following the rules of order, we were ready to put our feet on some very stiff necks to make shit happen.

CHAPTER 1
War

NERO

April, This Year - Detroit, Michigan

S*ometimes an end is just the beginning.*

The death of a loved one.

The end of a toxic relationship.

Unfortunately, I'd experienced both too many times to name. Tragedy often happened in cycles. Years of bliss, followed by periods of crushing blows. The simple fact of life was … there was only twenty-four hours in a day. Would I spend that precious time wallowing or winning? In everything, every calamity, every disappointment, I had no choice but to dust myself off and figure my shit out—whether it was making a hard decision, planning a move, or even celebrating the destruction of something harmful to me.

The bulldozer crushed the first wall of my childhood home in the Fitzgerald neighborhood near Puritan Street. The local church at the end of the street had partnered with a local construction company to buy up the abandoned houses near their building. Over recent years, there had been a push to rebuild and repurpose several dilapidated properties for families. Up until now, they'd been able to simply gut the properties because the structures were solid. Unfortunately, our old house was the first one they had to demolish.

It was bittersweet, watching my mother's house crumble to the ground. While the place held more bad memories than good, it was still hers. She'd worked hard to purchase that home. And we'd had a comfortable life there.

Looking at the remains of the house now, it was obvious that the subsequent owners or renters hadn't taken care of it. Before the demolition had started, the contractor allowed me a chance to walk through the home. I had immediately regretted my decision when I'd noticed the destruction inside—trash littering the floor, glass scattered everywhere. Thieves had stolen the copper piping, the old appliances, and even the toilets out of the house. After I exited the house, the putrid smell still clung to me. I wasn't sure why I even wanted to go inside, but it was something I needed to do. The end of a chapter in my life that felt unfinished.

As I scanned the area, I could almost hear the delighted screams of the kids I grew up with and the humming sound of bikes hitting the pavement. We'd spent hours running the street, climbing trees, building forts, shooting hoops, and doing shit that we shouldn't have been doing.

The construction crew continued their work as I forced myself back to a happier time in my life. If I concentrated hard, I could recall my mother's voice, the wheeze she always seemed to have, the spray of her inhaler, the sound of her shoes shuffling against the carpeted floor. Back then, I didn't understand why she moved so slow. I never even noticed that she was overweight. She was just Mom. Unfortunately, my mother had never really taken care of herself—smoking a pack of cigarettes every day, eating fried food most days, never exercising, always sitting in front of the television. She didn't monitor her blood sugar levels. She didn't even go to the doctor. And we all paid the price when she passed away in her sleep the day before my twelfth birthday.

Her death had changed my life in more ways than one. She had no living family, so I was separated from my brothers and sisters. They moved to Flint with their father, and since my dad had already died, Ace brought me to live with him.

My phone buzzed in my pocket. When I pulled it out, I frowned at the text from my office. The dean of the medical school had requested that I present my plans for the Juneteenth event at the staff forum. This afternoon. The Detroit chapter of the Mr. Black Organization had partnered with the Detroit NAACP and other local organizations to put on the annual Juneteenth Jubilee weekend festival.

I also managed to convince the university to sponsor a health fair on campus as part of the larger Juneteenth event. Several colleagues of mine had already volunteered to manage the booths, provide routine health screening, administer vaccines, perform mini-fitness classes, and entertain the youth through interactive games. And the medical school students would be on the ground assisting as well, which would in turn give them valuable experience in the field.

I responded to the text, letting my assistant know that I would return to the office shortly to tweak the slide deck I'd used to present my proposal to leadership months ago. With this change, I needed to forgo my lunch with Ace and make my way back to campus. I took one last look at my old house, before I headed to my car.

"Lil nigga!"

I stopped in my tracks, turning toward the voice. A man standing across the street waved at me.

"Dr. Bond," he called.

Eyeing him curiously, I noted his appearance. I couldn't see much from the distance, but I noticed the brown paper bag in one of his hands. Judging by the way he was holding it, I figured he had a bottle of liquor or a beer inside of the bag.

It had been years since I stepped foot on the block. Most of the punks I'd had beef with back then were long gone—some in jail, some dead, and some who left the hood behind for various reasons. This guy didn't appear threatening, though. And what the hell was he going to do anyway with the construction crew nearby and the plain-clothes police officer who'd been watching the activity all morning parked on the corner? I absently patted my side as I veered off my path toward the man. My gun was safe in its holster as always. Ace had always taught me to be smart and be watchful.

"Don't go looking for a fight but be ready for one."

His words echoed in my mind as I neared the man. I still couldn't make out his features, but he seemed familiar.

The stranger must have sensed my hesitation, so he said, "It's me. Walter King."

I blinked, stepping back to look at him fully. Sure enough, recognition finally dawned on me. "Yeah." Once I made it across the street, I reached out and shook his hand. "It's been a long time."

Walt smiled, flashing his rotted teeth. "It sure has. I kept up with you, though. I see Ace sometimes over at the barbershop."

My grandfather made it a point to show up in the community. He attended functions, donated to charities, and posted up at his brother's barbershop every Saturday. "He's still out there doing his thing," I said. "I keep telling him to slow his ass down."

"Nah, man. He's needed out here."

I studied Walt. Back in the day, he was known as a playa. He never went anywhere without his drumsticks. Always kept a girl on his arm. He was older than me, but he was like a big brother to us in the neighborhood. Had taught me how to play Michael Jackson's "Billie Jean" on the drums. Had even kept me out of serious trouble more than a few times.

"What's good with you?"

Walt scratched the side of his face, drawing my attention to his cracked skin. "Nothing much. I've been trying to find work, but it's been hard." I noticed that his eyes were dull, too. I couldn't see his feet because he had on sneakers, but his hands and ankles were swollen. The scar above his right eye seemed to be infected. "Ace told us that you're in Detroit now."

After my divorce, I accepted a faculty position at Wayne State University. I also moved my practice from Ann Arbor to Detroit. "I'm over at Henry Ford Health now."

He snapped his fingers. "That's what Ace said. What made you leave Ann Arbor?"

"My ex-wife," I joked. "Nah, I needed to come back to the city."

"Good. The city needs good doctors."

"Why don't you come and visit me?" I handed him my business card. "I can set you up for a physical with one of my colleagues. Maybe have someone look at that wound above your eye?"

He averted his gaze. "Nah, I'm good." He rubbed the cut with his thumb, and I cringed inwardly because his hands weren't clean. "I already had it checked out at the clinic."

I didn't believe him. I wasn't sure what he had going on health wise, but the unmistakable stench of crack smoke permeated from his clothes and his skin. I knew the smell well, since my father had spent the better part of his adult life strung out on the drug—until he died of an overdose when I was eight years old. I also knew the scent would follow me until I took a shower.

"Do you think you can spare a few dollars?" he asked. "I wanted to grab some nachos from the corner store."

My instinct was to tell him no because any money I'd give him would likely end up in his drug dealer's hands. But I pulled out a twenty-dollar bill anyway. Before I gave it to him, I said, "I know it might not seem important right now, but you really need to see a doctor about that cut above your eye."

He nodded. "I will. I'll ask my sister to bring me to the hospital to see you."

"Good." Again, I didn't believe him. But I sent up a silent prayer for him anyway and handed him the money.

Walt stuffed it in his pockets. "Thanks, Nero. You were

always one of the good ones. I always knew you'd do big things."

I swallowed past a hard lump in my throat. Seeing such a talented man succumb to the lure of a substance made me sad—and angry. "Take care of yourself, man."

I watched Walt amble away for a few seconds before I finally left. On my way back to my office, I grumbled a curse when my phone rang. When I didn't answer, my ex-wife called again. Then, again.

"What's up?" I said, finally picking up.

"It didn't have to be like this," Evelyn murmured. "I never wanted a divorce."

"Of course you didn't. You just wanted to step out on me whenever you felt like it and spend my money."

"You don't have that much money, Nero," she tossed back. "And you didn't really care who I slept with."

Life was an ongoing lesson. From the moment I'd married Evelyn, I realized that there were some things she was better off *not* knowing. Like the true size of my bank account. She'd always underestimated me, and I'd used that to my advantage when it was time to make my exit. "Did you call to talk about my money?" I asked pointedly.

"Can we talk about the house?"

It was the same argument we'd had since I filed for divorce. I graciously agreed to let her stay in the house rent-free for several years, as a form of spousal support. Her time was up. "It's a done deal, Evelyn. You knew this day was coming."

"Why don't you come over so we can talk?" she whined. "I told you the divorce wasn't the end for us."

I snickered. "Oh, it's absolutely over."

"What about Nala?"

Evelyn and I had married because she was pregnant with my youngest daughter, Nala—who was now twenty years old and attending Howard University. "I talked to her today," I said. "She's fine."

"But—"

"Zoe is too," I added. While Zoe wasn't Evelyn's biological daughter, the two were close. "She told me you two had lunch the other day, so I know you already knew that."

Evelyn muttered a curse. "I guess you've made up your mind."

"I did that seven years ago when I moved out and filed for divorce."

The carnage of our long marriage had only left me with resentment. I hated the fact that I'd even felt like I had no way other than down the aisle. I hated that I'd said those vows knowing I didn't love Evelyn. I hated that I wasted so much time being married to a woman I couldn't really stand. And I vowed years ago that I wouldn't spend another minute living a life that I didn't want. That was the day I moved out. The divorce was just a formality. Everything about us was wrong. From our philosophies to our taste in food to the way we viewed money and status.

"I ran into Dr. Jackson at an event the other day," she said. "He mentioned trying to woo you back to Michigan Medicine."

That wasn't going to happen. "I'll see him at the Juneteenth event in a couple of months. I'll be sure to let him know that I'm happy where I am." I sighed. "The real estate agent will be by today to put the sign up. Please cooperate with her."

"Nero, come on."

"I have to go," I told her before disconnecting the call.

Immediately, I dialed my real estate agent. Tamela Martin answered on the first ring. "Hi, Dr. Bond. Glad you called. I'm on my way to the house now to set the FOR SALE sign in the yard. I don't expect the house to remain on the market long."

"Thanks, Tamela. Let me know if you have any problems with my ex-wife."

"Sure thing," Tamela chirped. "By the way, are you available to meet me for lunch tomorrow? To discuss your current search? I found several properties in the city that you might be interested in."

When I moved back to Detroit, I purchased a condo in Midtown, closer to the hospital and the university. However, I had a desire to move into a single-family home with more space. On its surface, Tamela's offer was innocent. I knew that she had an ulterior motive, though. She'd been upfront with her romantic intentions, and I definitely planned to take her fine ass up on it—as soon as the deal was closed. Because I didn't fuck where I did business. Period. "How about we meet at the hospital?" I suggested. "Tomorrow is a clinic day, so I won't have much time."

"Sure," Tamela said, the disappointment in her voice evident.

"I'll check my calendar and get back to you this evening."

Arriving on campus, I parked and hurried into the office. After I spent an hour finalizing my presentation, I sent it off to the dean's admin so that she could add it to the larger slide deck. I took half an hour to grab a quick bite to eat before I made my way into the auditorium.

The forum started with introductions of the presenters, followed by an overview of the medical school, the staff, and the purpose of the meeting. As they segued into a research update, I checked my email. After I sent a follow-up message to a patient, I scanned my presentation one last time.

"This is the last time you steal from me, muthafucka."

The text had flashed across my screen right after the dean introduced the new chief financial officer and the topic had shifted to the medical school financial outlook. The recent reduction in federal funding had put several people on edge. Add to that, increased workloads and a reduced workforce, employees were downright hostile. Even so, I hadn't expected to receive the text. Especially from *her*.

I scanned the auditorium, hoping to catch a glimpse of the woman in question. Daphne Childs had always been professional. She was a well-respected, well-liked part of the team. Under her direction as facilities' director for the medical school, she'd earned a reputation for being fair, competent, and forward-thinking. As a result, her department had the lowest turnover rate at the university. Which was why her text was surprising.

My phone buzzed again. I glanced at the person sitting next to me, before opening the text thread.

Daphne: *I'll take your ass to court.*

Frowning, I scrolled up to reread some of the other texts I'd sent her in the past. Nothing in the few messages we'd exchanged warranted her response. While we'd worked together on the DEI committee for several months, we typically only ran into each other at forums like this or various after-work functions.

Daphne: *How dare you steal my shit*!

Someone's trying to punk me. I didn't have time for bullshit. If I did something to offend Daphne—or she thought I'd stolen from her—we needed to have a conversation.

Daphne: *You have messed with the wrong woman.*

I leaned forward, turning my head to my left, then to my right, still trying to find her in the crowd. Despite my earlier thoughts, in every interaction I'd had with Daphne, she'd struck me as the type of person who wasn't for the bullshit. She was direct, honest. I couldn't help but think the texts were coming from a very real place for her. *Who the hell hurt her?* And why did I want to hurt them? Was it her man? Her mama? Shit, I didn't know but I was invested now.

Daphne: *It's on sight when I see you.*

My thumb hovered over my phone. I was tempted to reply but wasn't sure what I'd say. I started and deleted a response at least three times before the CFO ended his speech. As the dean droned on about the need to buckle down on expenditures, his assistant gave me the cue to head to the stage. I made my way up to the front of the auditorium, scanning the crowd once again, hoping to see Daphne.

While Dean Powell read my bio and told the stupid-ass story about how we met years ago at a community event, I stepped onto the stage. Finally, I spotted her on the far-left side of the auditorium. She was whispering something to the woman sitting next to her. Instead of loose-fitting work attire, she wore a white, sleeveless blouse and a skirt. I couldn't see her shoes, but in my mind, she had on high-ass heels to accentuate those long-ass legs. Her hair wasn't braided, pulled back into a bun, or styled in a ponytail either. It was wild and free, framing her face perfectly. Decision made, I typed out a response to her last text message and hit SEND, just as Dean Powell called me over to the podium.

I launched into my presentation, giving a brief history lesson about the Juneteenth holiday and why it was important for the university to engage with its Black students, staff, and faculty. Then, I shared an overview of the jubilee, spending several minutes on the medical school's role in this year's event. As I hit all my bullet points, my gaze drifted over to Daphne once again, just as she glanced at her phone. Her eyes flashed to mine, and I smirked.

The message I sent had been short and to-the-point, with just enough nuance to keep the conversation either hot or cold. Her choice.

Me: *Will you keep your hair down for me? No ponytail holders allowed.*

CHAPTER 2
Think

DAPHNE

Yesterday

"That muthafucka took all my shit."

"What?" my bestie crowed. "Where are you?"

When I arrived home from my first vacation in years, I didn't expect to find my shit empty. That fool had taken the art on the walls, the dish towels, the blinds … I rushed through the house, checking rooms, opening drawers, and stepping into closets. The bathroom curtains. *Gone*. My rugs. *Not here*. And my brand new Tempur-Pedic mattress and bedroom set. *Nowhere in sight*. Yep. He took everything —all the televisions, my sofa, my mink coat, my designer handbags, my jewelry. Even my shoes weren't off-limits because he'd practically cleared out my shoe closet. Aside from my clothes, the only things he left were two chairs, the old recliner he kept in his bedroom, and his air mattress. Everything I'd worked for, everything I'd purchased when I bought my house last year … all my shit was gone.

Panic rose as I rushed through the house again, frantically searching for my feline best friend. "Kitty!" I called, checking in her favorite hiding spots. "Come on, baby! Come here!"

When Kitty didn't emerge after several minutes, I realized that material things weren't the only things he'd taken. The first tear fell before I realized it. Then, my legs gave out. Now on the floor, I picked up my phone. "Britt, he took everything." I ended the call, laid down on the floor, and cried.

An hour later, I was still in the same position, staring at nothing when I heard the jingle of keys in the door. Seconds later, my sister entered my house. I was the oldest of four—two girls and two boys. And at least seven foster siblings that had entered our lives at various times during my childhood. While most of them had hopped on the first plane or car out of Detroit the first chance they got, I stayed behind because I loved my city. Jada stayed behind because she was committed to preserving the appearance that her marriage was on solid ground, instead of shaky foundation.

Jada stopped in front of me, a hand on her hip and a scowl on her face. "I called the police."

"Why are you even here?" I muttered. "Especially since you obviously didn't check on Kitty while I was gone like you promised. If you had, you would've known she was gone."

From the time Jada entered my small world, she'd been

a thorn in my side. I'd recognized her toxicity as a kid, when she cried for hours because my parents bought *me* a birthday present. For all I knew, she *could've* come to my house, noticed my shit was gone, and shrugged it off because she just didn't give a fuck about anyone but herself. She was the worst kind of entitled, spoiled brat—the type of person I avoided at all costs. And, sister or not, I didn't fuck with her.

"Britt sent a text," she said, looking around the room.

I counted to ten. I was sure my best friend just panicked because she couldn't get to me, and wanted me to have support in the moment, but … *She knew better.* "Great."

"Are you sure it was him?"

"Who else would it be?" I asked incredulously.

She shrugged. "Maybe one of your many ex-boyfriends."

Raising a brow, I said, "You tried it." My sister was also the worst kind of Christian. Judgmental. Hypocritical. Holy on Sunday, and *Hoe*-ly every other day. The sheer audacity she always displayed pissed me off. "You really want to do this right now? You've been sneaking around with Deacon Community Dick for the last three years. Maybe your husband would be interested in a paternity test for my nephew?"

Jada bared teeth. "You shut up right now."

Closing my eyes, I rested my head against the wall. "Girl, go find you some friends and argue with them hoes. I don't have time for this shit. If you're not here to help, get the fuck out."

My parents were hard-working, extremely religious, and very giving people. We didn't have much, but they gave us a comfortable life. I honored them every day by checking in on them, cooking for them, buying their monthly groceries, and even paying a landscaper to keep their home the way my father liked it. But … I couldn't stand their daughter. That simple fact made family events uncomfortable for them. Mostly because she couldn't stop complaining about me to them. I, however, had a funky good time ignoring the fuck out of her at every barbecue, every celebration.

My bestie barreled into the house, sucking in deep breaths. She leaned against the wall. "Shit, I'm out of shape." Britt twisted her bohemian braids into a bun and scanned the living room. "You weren't lying." She met my gaze. "I'm so sorry, Daph." She looked at Jada. "Did you call the police?"

Jada glared at Britt. "Of course I did."

Britt and I had been joined at the hip since we skipped lunch at Vacation Bible School for Bomb Pops from the ice cream truck. Thirty years of enduring friendship, and she was more like a sister than the one currently staring back at me with disdain in her eyes.

I pinned Britt with a glare. "Why did you call her?"

Rolling her eyes, Britt shrugged. "I panicked. She was close, and I wasn't sure I would be able to get out of that hot-ass plant early. Besides, you gave her a key to check on the house while we were gone. I thought y'all were working on the relationship."

My best friend worked as a millwright for one of the big automotive companies. She started right after high school and had made a good life for herself, even going back to school to get her bachelor's degree on the company's dime. Britt was also a licensed residential builder and owned a development company. She invested thousands into the community by using her skills to rehab derelict neighborhoods in the Detroit area for Black families looking to move back to the city. It was a mission I fully supported.

Britt dropped her purse on the floor and trekked to the kitchen. Returning, she said, "He took your canned goods! Who does that? Times must be super hard if Campbell's Soup has resale value on the street. Every corner store in the hood has chicken noodle soup."

"Language," Jada warned.

"Evangelist, please. You can take your uptight ass to the church house and practice a congregational song or hop on that deacon's dick. I got Daphne."

Jada fumed. "Daphne is *my* sister, Britt. I will stay here until the police come."

Lifting my knees to my chest, I rested my forehead against my legs. "This is so stupid," I murmured, angry at the tears that hadn't stopped falling.

"I told you so," Jada said. "He's been trouble since we were kids. You let Mama guilt you into letting him stay here. Why didn't you change the locks when you kicked him out?"

Britt sat down next to me, wrapping her arms around me. Ignoring Jada, she wiped the tears from my cheeks. "You're going to be okay. He's a bitter-ass bum."

That *bitter-ass bum* was my cousin, Neil. We'd grown up like siblings because he was one of my parent's foster kids. When he fell on hard times, I gave him a place to land. It had worked in the beginning. I wasn't lonely, but it felt good to have someone to talk to when I got off work, to have someone to eat dinner with a few nights a week.

After six months of sleeping in one of my bedrooms, though, he stopped paying rent. Even then, I didn't kick him out. I wasn't hurting for money, and I had a heart for his struggle. I knew firsthand what it felt like to start over after a breakup, and his ex-wife had taken him through the wringer. But … Neil was a con man, a professional thief. He scammed for a living, stealing appliances out of vacant homes, copper from power grids, and thousands of dollars from vulnerable elderly women.

After Christmas, I noticed that a few pieces of crystal from my curio cabinet were missing. And when my grandmother's elephant broach disappeared, I knew it was time for him to go. A few months ago, he moved out, and I immediately changed the locks. I still wasn't sure how he managed to get through my security system, but Neil was gifted in many areas, especially cyber security. He wouldn't have had a hard time hacking my system.

Sucking in a deep breath, I finally stood and dusted myself off. I didn't have time to wallow or whine. I needed a stiff drink and a plan. I glanced at Jada. "Thanks for coming, but you can go now." I turned to Britt. "Call James. I need his help."

Britt gave me a quizzical look. "Are you sure?"

My ex-boyfriend—*her older brother*—was a security expert. While I didn't like him as a person anymore, he knew his shit. "I don't have a choice. I can't live here and not feel safe." I gestured to the empty room around me. "I'll file my insurance claim, replace my things, but Neil could just as easily come back and do it again. I'm not gonna run from this … or him. I'll just be ready for his ass." I stomped toward my bedroom. "Bye, Jada."

Today

I LOVED MY JOB. As a facilities director, I planned, organized, and coordinated all medical school facilities and catering operations. My days consisted of meetings, management of my talented staff, making recommendations for space use, and developing proposals for leadership. Basically, keeping our occupants happy and our research operation profitable.

Most days, I enjoyed interacting with people, catching up over coffee in the kitchenette, and conducting tours for prospective faculty candidates. However, returning from vacation to an empty house, inept police assistance, and countless calls from my extended family and my parents imploring me to take pity on my wayward cousin, had put me in a foul mood.

I looked good, though. Britt had spent the night at my place and forced me to dress up for work instead of donning my comfortable work attire. She even convinced me to show some skin. After all, I'd spent a whole week in a tropical paradise. My body was refreshed, and I still had that vacation glow.

Sometime after my third meeting of the morning, I realized that as much as I loved my career, there was one thing I hated about work—dealing with colleagues. People who thought I didn't know what the hell I was doing, faculty who thought I worked for them and not the university, and the unrealistic expectations of department heads who had no concept of a budget. And I'd encountered at least fifteen of those types of people in a matter of hours.

The rumors had run rampant that the university was preparing to crack down on spending because of a projected deficit for the next fiscal year. Staff were concerned about layoffs, faculty were worried about their research, and I was tired of using scotch tape to hold our aging buildings together.

To avoid cussing someone out, I ate my lunch in my office, hoping to find a moment of peace before the staff forum. My phone buzzed on the table. I glanced at the screen and rolled my eyes. *I guess peace is not on the agenda.*

"Hey," I said.

My brother's voice came through the receiver. "What's up, sis?"

"Work," I replied, popping a blueberry in my mouth. My brother rarely called unless he wanted something, so I wouldn't hold my breath expecting anything different today. "What's going on, Dre?"

"I need a favor."

Big surprise. My parents had raised all of us to be self-sufficient, but for some reason, my siblings thought I was the Bank of Childs. My brother had moved to Texas, under the guise of getting his act together, but had been in my pockets every month since he relocated. Granted, I was the only one he could ask. My sister had never really worked and was solely dependent on her cheating-ass husband to fund her lifestyle. I suspected she'd even borrowed money from me through our parents, too.

"What do you need?" I asked.

"Can I borrow five hundred until the end of the month? I had an emergency. Couldn't be helped. I'll send the money back as soon as I get paid. Promise."

"I guess you haven't heard."

"What?"

"Your cousin robbed me while I was on vacation. My money is tied up right now. Have to replace most of my shit."

"Who? Neo?"

The family had referred to Neil by his nickname almost exclusively since he was a baby. "Yep," I confirmed. "He even stole Kitty." The police had told me I shouldn't expect to get my cat back, and that shit hurt. Kitty had been with me for five years. She was family. I swallowed as fresh tears filled my eyes. Clearing my throat, I added, "I'm pressing charges, too." *If they ever find his ass.*

"Damn, sis. That's messed up."

"Right."

"Well, can you give me two hundred?" Dre asked.

Maybe it's time to block him. At least until I was in a better mind state to deal with his bullshit. "I don't have it," I lied.

"Can you take it from your savings?" he pressed.

"Boy, bye."

"Wait," he said. "I'm sorry. I know I'm wrong for that. You're going through a lot right now and I'm being insensitive."

I ate the final piece of my sandwich while he offered several excuses for his behavior. *His* life, *his* unemployment check, *his* new girlfriend, and *his* child support.

"I wish I could come there and help you out," he added.

So I can have another trifling man in my guest room? Hell. No. "You're doing what you need to do. Down in Texas."

"For what it's worth, Neo was probably desperate. Probably messed with the wrong nigga and got scared."

I took a measured breath. "I don't care about his problems."

"All I'm sayin is … y'all need to talk. Come to an understanding."

"Oh, I understand." I balled up my trash and threw it in the wastebasket under my desk. "I understand that there's no coming back from this. Fuck him."

"Daph, come on. You're better—"

I hung up on him. I didn't want to hear that I was better than this from anyone else. Neo had made it very clear that he didn't give a damn about our history. So I would act accordingly and treat him like I treated everyone I didn't fuck with anymore. Like dust.

A few minutes later, I gathered my tablet and headed toward the auditorium. On my way there, I stopped at a kiosk and ordered an iced coffee. I had ten minutes to spare, so I sat down on one of the couches and drafted an email to my boss. Although I'd just returned from vacation, I needed to take additional time off to clear my head. I was no good to my staff or myself in this state.

Before I could hit SEND on the email, I heard someone call my name. I scanned the room and smiled at my co-worker, Lanelle. "Hey, girl."

Lanelle hurried over to me and sat on the couch. "You're back."

"I'm back," I repeated sarcastically. "Ready to go on another vacation."

"I know!" She cracked up. "I'm like that every single time I go out of town. I need a vacation from my vacation."

We caught up for a few minutes, before she said, "You know they're talking cuts now."

I nodded grimly. The budget situation was concerning on many fronts. While I managed my department well, I desperately needed to add new staff due to the increased demands. The last thing I wanted was to *lose* someone. "I heard. I just hope I don't have to withdraw my requests for new project managers."

Lanelle was the Associate Director of Budget for the Med School. Over the years, we'd created an alliance of likeminded Black women on the job and had supported each other through some crazy shit. We'd also developed a friendship and had been there for each other through personal trials. "I'm fighting for you, sis," she assured me.

I thanked her. "Glad you're in the room."

We stood and made our way to the auditorium. "Let's get drinks soon," she suggested. "I have to tell you about this guy I met online."

"I'm down. I need several drinks."

Lanelle eyed me curiously. "Why? You should be relaxed and refreshed."

"You just don't know," I grumbled.

As we made our way to our seats, I gave her a quick rundown of what had happened. The meeting started, and we were still whispering to each other as the dean finished his spiel. Just telling her about it made me even angrier. So angry that I fired off a text to my cousin.

Me: *This is the last time you steal from me, muthafucka.*

Even after the new CFO of the medical school took the stage, I was so angry that I sent more texts, and even issued a threat.

Me: *It's on sight when I see you.*

The dean returned to the podium and read the bio of Dr. Nero Bond. Lanelle shushed me as she gazed at the stage. I wasn't surprised because several of the women at work wanted a taste of the elusive doctor. According to one of my friends who worked as a nurse at the hospital, his patients loved him. He was respected by students and faculty, had always presented himself well, and didn't look like the typical stuffy or weird professor. He dressed like he was down for the cause. It wasn't uncommon for him to wear a hoodie and sneakers into the classroom. We hadn't interacted much, but he definitely had that swag.

Unlike Lanelle, though, I wasn't interested in him. I preferred to keep my work interactions professional. I never dated colleagues. The last thing I needed was on-the-job drama.

"I think I'm going to leave," I whispered.

Lanelle's gaze was transfixed on the stage. "No, stay. When he's done, we can leave."

Dr. Bond started is speech, and I settled into my seat, trying my best to pay attention. It helped that the subject mattered to me. *Juneteenth*. The holiday *and* the jubilee event. As he started his speech, I glanced at my phone and unlocked it. Pressing the Messages app, I gasped. All along, I thought I had been sending those texts to *Neo*. But, no … My dumbass had sent them to *Nero*. I looked up at him, only to find him staring right back at me, a mischievous smirk on his sexy-as-fuck lips. *Oh shit.*

I swallowed, pulling my eyes away from him and back to the text. I reread the text I'd sent just before. Then, I read all the messages again. I slumped down in my seat, suddenly uncomfortable and more embarrassed than I'd ever been.

As I tried to think of an efficient way to handle this situation, I listened as he went over the details of the health fair the university would be hosting on campus in partnership with Henry Ford Hospital and the Mr. Black Organization. I thought about all the people it could help. For years, my parents didn't even have a primary care doctor. The only time they'd received medical care was during an emergency. I knew several people who had that same philosophy, and it was killing our community. A few hours ago, I would've offered my assistance to Dr. Bond because I believed in the cause. But now …

Yeah, I'm not going near him.

Nero ended his speech, and the room stood and applauded him. I begrudgingly joined them, standing up and clapping. When he exited the stage, he made eye contact with me again. The smirk was still there, and … *Dr. Bond is fine as hell.* It was almost like he knew my thoughts because he smiled. *Shit, that's beautiful.* Almost like the sun.

And his intense gaze was doing things to my body that should've been reserved for someone who didn't work with me. Someone that hadn't been on the receiving end of several threatening messages. I'd made a complete fool of myself and—I'd already made up my mind—I was absolutely going to pretend I didn't even know Dr. Bond. *At least for a few months.*

As the meeting dragged on, I stared at the text he'd sent.

Nero: *Will you keep your hair down for me? No ponytail holders allowed.*

Finally, I'd had enough. I sent that email to my boss. Because I needed a break—from work, from my fucked-up life, and now from Nero's smile.

CHAPTER 3

I Can't Get Next to You

NERO

I *should've* taken Daphne's mortified glance after she read my message as my cue to leave it alone. Obviously, she'd mistakenly sent me the texts. I could tell by her wide-eyed response to my text, the way she'd slumped in her chair, and the fact that she'd done everything she could to avoid meeting my gaze. That look in her eyes read "I fucked up" more than "you stole my shit."

I *should've* responded by sending her an assuring text, letting her know that I was just kidding with her.

I *should've* explained that my intent was to make her laugh.

What I shouldn't have done was send that damn response in the first place. I definitely shouldn't have smiled at her the way I had. Sure, I could pass it off as genuine concern, but I knew what I was thinking. *She's beautiful.* Which led me to the next thing I shouldn't have done—

stayed until the meeting ended when I'd never done that before. *I also shouldn't be thinking about her at all.* So, there's that.

Fridays were for poker, food, beer, or sleep. After the week I'd had, I had planned to enjoy all of the above. Yet instead of returning to my office, packing my bag, and driving my ass home to start the weekend, I waited outside of the auditorium as people exited. For her.

The last thing I needed was drama. Or misunderstandings. Or questions about my professionalism. My decision to wait for her served two purposes. One, to assure her I didn't mean anything by my words. And two, to assure myself that she was alright. *And that I'm not really attracted to her.*

As I stood there, arms folded across my chest, eyes focused on the door and not the people trying to get my attention, I grew more irritated with myself than anything. Because I didn't do this type of shit. I didn't play games, and I damn sure didn't send suggestive text messages to colleagues. Still … there was something about Daphne, something about the tone of her texts that intrigued me. I couldn't stop myself from wanting to know more about her situation, more about her.

"Nero!" Dean Powell grinned as he walked toward me. "I'm pleasantly surprised at the response we're getting for the health fair. The board is thrilled, and the students are excited. It'll be a good opportunity for our cohorts to gain valuable experience in a fun and educational way. Thank you for considering our campus for the health fair."

"I had a lot of help," I told him. Planning the health fair had consumed my free time for months. The logistics alone had caused many sleepless nights. But it was worth it to hear my students spreading the word to their friends and families who hadn't made health and wellness a priority. "I hope you'll make it down to campus that day, Elijah."

He stammered a bit trying to come up with an excuse not to be in attendance. It was unfortunate, though, because Elijah had served as Mr. Black Detroit many years ago, prior to rising the ranks within the university. Once he was appointed Dean of the Medical School, though, he'd changed. He'd even resigned from the organization. Suddenly, *our* struggle was no longer *his* struggle.

"I know you understand," he explained. "It's graduation season and my wife would kill me if I missed my niece's party."

I understood Elijah was full of shit. He wasn't the only one. University Leadership talked a good game, but many of them had no intention of supporting the event with their presence—or even with a monetary donation. Some people had no idea why Juneteenth was a holiday. Some wanted to forget about it. Some couldn't care less about Black freedom.

Elijah clasped my shoulder. "I'll have my assistant put a lunch meeting on your calendar. So we can catch up and you can finally let me know if you want to accept that offer."

"Sounds like a plan." A few weeks ago, I was offered a Vice Chair role for the Diversity, Equity, and Inclusion team. And I'd purposely delayed my answer because I wasn't sure I wanted to add to my already full plate. I didn't mind serving, but my schedule was out of control between my practice at the hospital, primary care at a local clinic, teaching, my research, and the countless committees that needed my time. Virtual visits had made my job easier to an extent, but the bulk of my patients required in-person attention.

Daphne finally strolled out of the auditorium, head

down, brows furrowed, and eyes on her phone, and I found myself distracted by her. I didn't even realize Elijah was still talking until he called my name.

"Are you okay?" he asked curiously.

"I'm fine."

Daphne smiled at Lanelle, who'd just whispered something in her ear. The man who joined them looked familiar, but I couldn't place him. He also leaned in a little too close to her. The two women laughed heartily for whatever reason. The guy rubbed her shoulder, his finger lingering on her shoulder too long.

Elijah's voice cut through my eavesdropping. "Did you hear what I said?"

I blinked. *No.*

Daphne hugged ol' boy with the faded khakis on. *Looking like a lame-ass Jake from State Farm.*

"Anyway," Elijah continued, "I was thinking we—"

"Excuse me," I interrupted when Daphne walked toward the bay of elevators by herself. "I just remembered I need to take care of something. I'll get back with you Monday."

I walked away without another word and easily caught up to her. "Daphne?"

She stopped in her tracks, then turned around slowly. But when she realized it was me, her smile faded, and her eyes widened slightly. "I would look really crazy if I ran from you, right?"

I chuckled. "Really crazy."

Closing her eyes, she sighed. "Honestly, I thought you would be gone by now."

"You thought?" I asked, raising a brow.

"More like hoped," she answered truthfully. She folded her arms over her chest. "I guess you're here about the text messages."

"Sort of."

She frowned. "What does that mean?"

Damn. Has she always been this beautiful? Or was I trippin'? I struggled to remember what I'd planned to tell her once I spoke to her, so I winged it. "I figured the text messages were a mistake," I said. "Since I'm pretty sure you already had a bad day, I thought I would let you off the hook—so that you won't sink into your chair or hide behind a piece of paper the next time I see you." A soft smile formed on her lips, but she didn't say anything, so I kept going. "If you want me to handle the bum who stole from you, I'm down for that, too."

Daphne's eyes flashed to mine. She studied me for a moment before she asked, "Is that so?"

My gaze dropped to her lips. "I don't say things I don't mean."

"Thank you, but I'll handle it. It's a family issue."

"So your man didn't steal from you?"

She shook her head. "If my man had stolen from me, I'd be in jail right now."

"Ah." I wanted to know if she had a man, but I wouldn't ask because it really wasn't my business. *Even though I want it to be.*

"I don't have a man," she offered, scratching the back of her neck.

I nodded. "Are you okay?"

"Other than being completely embarrassed and having to basically start over, I'm good."

"If there's anything you need …" I let the sentence hang in the air, because I didn't trust myself not to ask her out.

She eyed me skeptically. "We don't really know each other like that."

"Maybe I *want* to know you like that?" I shot back, before I could stop myself.

"Why?" she breathed, her voice low.

After years of not giving a fuck about relationships, becoming a girl dad had shifted things for me, made me strive for something other than getting lost inside of a wet pussy. Engaging in hit-it-and-quit-it relationships had ceased being a thing the moment I looked into Zoe's eyes. Because I knew I would want to kill anyone who treated her like I'd treated women in the past.

Marrying Evelyn was my misguided attempt of being a better man, a better father. Unfortunately, I learned a valuable lesson during my time with her. *A person can make shit worse trying to do the right thing.* By the time I finally divorced her, I told myself that I wouldn't invite just any random woman into my space. Except … *Daphne isn't random.* And now I was rethinking my vow to never fuck where I did business.

Smirking, I replied, "Because I like your hair."

Daphne laughed. "You're silly for that."

"I'm serious," I countered. While I wasn't sure what had happened to make me want to abandon my own rules of conduct for workplace relationships, I absolutely planned to roll with it. "Have dinner with me?"

Her mouth fell open. "What?"

"Dinner?"

"I …" She tucked a strand of her hair behind an ear. "As in a date?"

I hunched a shoulder. "As in dinner," I said matter-of-factly. "Just food."

"Nero, this is crazy."

"Not really. We've eaten a meal together before."

"With ten other people," she pointed out.

I scanned the area. "Want me to invite ten people?" I

spotted another colleague of ours nearby. "We can ask Oliver to join us."

I opened my mouth to speak, but Daphne shushed me. "You better not call him over here. You know I can't stand that fool."

"Me neither," I confessed.

She laughed. "You got jokes, huh?"

"Sometimes."

Her phone buzzed, and she glanced at it. Her smile slipped. "Shit," she grumbled.

"Is everything okay?"

Ignoring me, she tapped at the screen, presumably sending a text. When she finished, she said, "I can't go out to dinner with you, Nero." She sighed. "You're cool, but this is weird. And I think it's best we keep things on a professional level."

Damn. It wasn't what I wanted to hear, but I wouldn't question her. "I understand. I meant what I said earlier, though. If I can do anything to help, let me know."

She flashed a sad smile. "Thanks." Turning, she headed for the elevator. When the door open, she glanced back at me one last time and then stepped inside. Seconds later, she walked out and headed back to me. "How about a drink?"

A smile tugged at my lips. "I'm down for whatever you want."

Pointing at me, she said, "*Just* a drink."

I held up my arms. "Got it."

"And I'll meet you there."

"Where is *there* exactly?"

Daphne cracked up. "You asked me out. Surprise me. I just need an hour to finish up here."

"I'm good with that. I'll text you the location." Unable to resist, I leaned in, catching a whiff of her perfume. It was subtle, yet sexy. Delicate, but strong. Feminine. Just like her. "Just a reminder … no ponytail holders allowed."

"YOU BETTER BE GLAD I," Daphne hurled her axe, hitting just below the bullseye on the wood target, "keep a spare outfit and shoes in my car."

I marked her score. "I don't even want to think about why you keep a whole suitcase in your trunk."

Drinks had turned into dinner, followed by axe throwing at a venue in Corktown, the oldest neighborhood in Detroit. The area had a historical feel to it, which was partly due to the cobblestone surface on Michigan Avenue. The city had spent a lot of money revitalizing the area to attract more visitors and to entice potential residents to move close to downtown. As a result of the investment, the community was bustling with several restaurants and bars, shops, and even a boutique hotel.

She smirked. "Trust me, you don't want to know."

After stepping up to the lane, I threw my axe, hitting the bullseye.

She grumbled a curse but gave me a high-five anyway. "I think you lied when you told me you'd never done this before."

"Nah, you just assumed I didn't know what I was doing. I told you I hadn't been *here* before."

Daphne shook her head. "You tricked me." She shoved me playfully before tossing her axe, once again missing the bullseye. "Damnit."

I squeezed her shoulders. "It's okay to admit defeat. I promise I won't tell anyone."

She sat down at the high-top table behind the lane and

took a sip of her cocktail. "You better not. I have a rep to protect."

After I took my turn, I joined her at the table and ordered another round of drinks. "I think you owe me something."

Craning her neck to check the score, she glared at me. "Again! Are you on a league or something?"

I rested my elbows on the table. "I'm just good. At pretty much everything."

She followed suit, leaning forward, eyes on mine. Raising a challenging brow, she asked, "Everything?"

The air changed around us as we stared at each other. The table was small, so it wouldn't have been a stretch to kiss her. But Ace had taught me to always follow a woman's cues and let her take the lead. And I had a feeling she was leading to something I was down with. "I told you …" I raked my gaze over her face, searching her eyes, mentally tracing the line of her nose, and finally zeroing in on her full lips. "I always mean what I say."

Daphne blew out a slow breath, but she didn't retreat, didn't even flinch. And I tried to act nonchalant and unaffected while simultaneously envisioning her legs around me as I fucked the shit out of her against the wood target. Her eyes dropped to my mouth, but she blinked, seemingly snapping herself out of something.

After clearing her throat, she changed the subject. "So, are you going to tell me how you know how to throw an axe?"

"Full disclosure. My daughters took me axe throwing for my birthday last year."

"Just once?"

"And I grew up in an environment where I had to learn how to hit a target. Whether it was with a bottle, a knife, or a gun."

A smile played on her lips. “I’m not usually surprised by people, but you have definitely thrown me for a loop today, Nero.”

“Why is that?”

She eyed me over the rim of her glass. “Because you didn’t make me feel like shit for cussing your ass out earlier. Or like I was an angry, Black woman. Since then, you’ve done nothing but make me laugh and respect my boundaries.”

“Did you think I was an asshole?”

Daphne nearly choked on her drink, then burst out in a fit of giggles. “No. I know you’re not an asshole. But working on a project, serving with you on a committee, attending some of the same functions, is not the same as spending one-on-one time together.”

“Is this your way of telling me you want me to take you out again?”

She nibbled on her bottom lip. “Maybe.”

I leaned in, brushing my palm over hers. “But …”

“We do work together. I have rules.”

I inched closer. “Me too.”

“I didn’t expect to feel so drawn to you. I really enjoyed myself tonight.”

“Me too,” I repeated.

“We’re adults,” she added.

“Exactly.” I bumped her nose with mine, just to test the waters a little more. “And you’re beautiful and sexy and …” I kissed the corners of her lips, then ran my tongue over her bottom lip, enjoying her sharp intake of breath. “I want you.”

“No promises,” she breathed.

“Nah,” I agreed. “Just … tonight.”

Daphne gripped my collar with her fist. “I’m good with that.”

I kissed her then, gripping her chin with my palm, holding her to me as I explored her mouth. The buzz around us—the loud chatter, the sound of axes hitting the wood, the music—dulled to a tiny roar. And I realized that if I didn't get her out of there, I wouldn't be able to stop myself from pulling her onto my lap.

I broke the kiss finally, took a few deep breaths, and scanned the area. "Let's go."

Twenty minutes later, we entered a suite at the nearby Shinola Hotel. With our mouths fused together, we stumbled toward the bed, nearly tripping over a chair.

Daphne pulled my belt off, unbuttoned my pants, and pushed them down. I tugged at her blouse, and she pulled it off. But when she went to remove her bra, I placed my hand over hers. "Leave it on."

If I thought Daphne was beautiful with clothes on, I didn't even have a word to describe her without her clothes. *Exquisite. Stunning*. Dropping to my knees, I kissed her stomach, dipped my tongue in her navel, and licked my way down to the waistband of her jeans. "Turn around," I murmured against her brown skin.

Daphne pulled back, her eyes almost black with desire. But she did as she was told. My gaze lowered to her ass. Unable to resist, I grabbed her butt with my palms, and sunk my teeth into the flesh.

"Shit," she murmured.

Chuckling, I pulled her panties down. "You like that?"

"Yes," she breathed. "More of that, please."

I stood, spinning her around to face me. Gripping her hips, I lifted her up and dropped her on the bed. Slowly, I crawled over her, kissing my way up her body and burying my face in her pussy, licking her slit and sucking her clit into my mouth. I couldn't get enough of her, and when her first orgasm hit her, I didn't even wait before going in for more. The way she groaned, the way she dug her nails into my scalp, the way she begged for more, made me want to give everything to her.

Daphne climaxed again, shuddering beneath me. Once I slipped on the condom, she beckoned to me with her forefinger. "Come here."

I rested my weight on her.

Peering at me through hooded lids, she smiled. "I definitely like that." She rubbed her finger over my lips before she kissed me again.

It had been years since I spent time just kissing someone. But I found myself wanting her mouth on mine, her tongue against mine. In my marriage, most of our interaction revolved around money and sex. We didn't talk nor spend time together. There were no vacations or date nights. I paid the bills, and she spent my money.

Daphne bit down on my lip. "This is okay, right?"

I sucked her tongue into my mouth and pressed my dick to her pussy. "Hmmm …"

She purred, bucking against me. "We're going to be okay in the morning?"

"Absolutely," I murmured against her lips as I thrust inside of her. She felt so good, so warm, so wet, I had to steel myself against the sensations flooding through me. I wanted to take my time, but I also wanted to come. No, I *needed* to come.

Her eyes fluttered closed. "Yes," she whispered, biting down on my shoulder.

That was all I needed. We took our time, pushing and pulling, giving and taking in equal measure. We were good together, in sync with each other. And I found myself thinking ahead to more nights like this, more time with her.

As our pace quickened, I realized I was unraveling,

losing control. In the past, that would've scared me, but I wanted to lean into it, let things happen organically. I thrust into her once, twice, then two more times before she came, squeezing my hips with her long legs and my dick with her pussy. It felt so good, so right, I followed her over swiftly, with her name on my lips and her face seared on my brain.

We stayed like that, arms and legs entangled for a moment before I rolled off of her. Pulling her close to me, I brushed my lips over her brow, reveling in the fact that she didn't protest. She nuzzled her nose into my neck.

"I'm tired." She tugged my earlobe into her mouth. "But not ready for the night to end."

"No worries." I placed her hand against my growing erection. "I'm good with that, too."

We spent the rest of the night exploring each other, learning more about one another. It was irrational, the way I wanted her. We'd only spent one evening together, but I knew from the moment she glanced at the menu earlier and decided to order food instead of drinks that I wanted it to be more dates, more days. It wasn't that she ordered the Henny Chops, a side of seasoned fries, and a spicy margarita. It was the way she didn't pretend not to be hungry. It was the way she listened intently when I talked and offered her viewpoint with no qualms about it. It was the way we fist bumped each other when we agreed on something and defended our viewpoints when we disagreed. Always respectful, never attempting to change each other's minds. She was a breath of fresh air, for sure. Intelligent. Intense. Irresistible. *And I want more of this.*

CHAPTER 4

I Wanna Be Where You Are

DAPHNE

I bit down on the only thing I could find. My arm. It had finally happened. I'd lost my mind. How else could I explain my current predicament?

Skirt hiked up.

Legs in the air.

Nero's dick in my pussy.

Nero's thumb on my clit.

In his office.

Shit. It was my place of employment, too. I was pretty sure his assistant knew what was up when I'd shown up two days last week and one day this week for lunch. With no food in sight. But damnit … It felt too good to stop. No matter how inappropriate it was. No matter how bad this would look if any of his colleagues, his staff, or his students walked in on us.

This was the way it had been, though, since he'd beat

me at axe throwing and then fucked me until I could barely move at a hotel in the city. His skill in the bedroom had rendered me silly and horny. *And thirsty*. I couldn't think about why now, because …

I'm coming. And I couldn't scream. I couldn't groan. The only thing I could do was grunt. Softly. The delicious orgasm—the second of the day—rolled through me, and I was helpless to do anything but let it take over.

When it was over, I opened my eyes to find Nero staring down at me, a mischievous smirk on his lips.

"You good?" he whispered, a hint of amusement in his eyes.

I nodded, struggling to catch my breath. "I'm fine. Are you?"

He bent down and captured my lips in a searing kiss. "Better than good."

My stomach tightened as he started the dance again, winding me back up like a rag doll, taking me higher with each thrust, until another orgasm crested within me. But, this time, we came together.

I lifted myself up on my elbows and glanced at him. "I definitely have a problem."

Nero helped me get dressed, sucking my nipples through my bra as he zipped up my skirt, nibbling on my earlobe as he buttoned my blouse, and pressing his growing erection into my stomach as he trailed wet kisses over my collarbone, up my neck, to my lips. "What's that?" he murmured against my mouth.

I gripped his hair in my fist and kissed him. Hard. "You."

The corners of his mouth quirked up. "I'm a problem now?" He tugged me forward, against the hard ridge of his dick. "I tend to think of myself as your solution."

I cracked up. "You're so corny." Yet, even as I said it, I

knew it was a lie. Nero was everything but corny. Thoughtful. Smart. Sexy. Despite the whole debacle surrounding that crazy-ass text, I enjoyed being with him, getting to know him. Which made me sorta grateful that I couldn't control my temper that day in the auditorium. We'd spent the last two weeks immersed in each other and I couldn't regret it.

It wasn't just sex either. We talked. *A lot.* He shared some things about his childhood, and I told him about my upbringing in the church and the fractured relationship I had with my sister. Nero listened when I unexpectedly burst into tears while explaining the reason why I'd sent the text message that day. And he'd even suggested we drive to Neil's old hood to find him.

"Did you think about what I asked?" Nero brushed my hair away from my shoulder and licked the base of my neck. "About tomorrow?"

Nero had asked me to join him at a faculty event, but I wasn't sure I was ready to walk into a room on his arm. This thing between us was still new and I preferred to keep it quiet for a while. The last thing I needed was to become the topic of the weekly gossip that tended to spread around the building like a wildfire. I bit down on my bottom lip. "Do I have to?"

"No," he told me.

Tilting my head, I observed him. He was almost too good to be true. When we started this, we promised to be honest with each other. And he'd stuck to it. Nero never asked me to do anything I wasn't comfortable with, which was in stark contrast to the men I dated in the past. "Are you sure you're not disappointed?"

He brushed his finger over my jawline. "I'm good with whatever you decide."

I believed him, but I still felt like shit. "I'm just not

ready for that." Hell, I hadn't even told Britt about this. "I kind of like that we're keeping this quiet for now."

Placing his finger over my mouth, he whispered, "It's okay, Daphne. You don't have to explain."

Shit, I love the way he says my name. "You mean that, don't you?"

He opened the small refrigerator in his office and pulled out a bag from Panera Bread. "Absolutely," he said, passing the bag to me. "I figured we should actually eat today."

Opening it, I gasped. "How did you know I loved the Strawberry Poppyseed Salad?"

"I overheard you the other day talking to Lanelle about it in the cafeteria. Figured I would surprise you."

I peered up at him, torn between eating my salad and climbing on his lap. "Thank you." In the end, my stomach made the decision when it growled.

Nero joined me on the small loveseat he kept in his office. He pulled another salad out of the bag. As we ate, he told me more about the upcoming Juneteenth Jubilee. "I'll be glad when it's over. Planning events is not my thing."

I popped a blueberry in my mouth. "Will you have to plan the event next year, too?"

He'd already explained his role in the Mr. Black Organization to me but had stopped short of giving specific details about his responsibilities. I already knew a little bit about the org because my father was a member for years, so it was interesting to hear about their efforts in the community now. "I have another two years," he replied. "Then, we'll select another person to take over the mantle."

"That's cool. How did you get into this?"

"Ace."

Nero's grandfather, Ace, was a legendary hero in certain parts of the city. Even though I grew up on a different side of town, I heard tall tales about the Bond family. Some of the kids in my neighborhood had likened them to the mob. As a kid, I had actively prayed to never run into one of them. "I still can't believe you're one of *those* Bonds," I mused.

He chuckled. "Ironic, huh?" He leaned forward and kissed me softly. "Not only did you run into one of us, you also just let me fuck you in my office." He took a bite of his salad and smirked. "And you would probably let me do it again if you didn't have to go back to work."

I pointed my fork at him. "True."

Nero barked out a laugh. "See. I knew it." He finished his salad and rested his back against the sofa. "It's been a long time since I've done this," he admitted.

I stared at his profile, memorizing the lines of his face. His brown skin was so smooth, so soft, I couldn't help but nuzzle my nose against his cheek. I set my salad on the table and leaned back against him, pleasantly surprised when he wrapped his arm around me. "You haven't eaten lunch in a long time?" I teased.

He brushed his mouth over my temple. "After Nala graduated from elementary school, Evelyn and I never shared a meal together again."

"Really?" Nero had mentioned his ex-wife a few times. Each instance, he made it clear that there was nothing more between him. Not because he said those words, but because he didn't seem to like her at all.

"Not alone anyway," he amended. "Shit, even before that."

"Did you ever love her?"

"I cared for her," he said. "I wouldn't say it was love."

"Why did you stay?"

"Because I thought it was the right thing to do. I married her when she was pregnant with Nala, and I already had custody of Zoe. I just figured it was best to be together. So that my girls could grow up in the same house."

The more he told me about his life, the more I wanted to learn. "I love your bond with your daughters." Nero had never shied away from telling me about his family. Even the not-so-good parts like the death of his parents and how he came to live with his grandfather. It was clear that he adored his girls and was proud of the women they'd become. "Sometimes I wonder if I missed out on something special by not having kids," I offered.

"Why didn't you?"

I let out a slow breath. "Because my parents brought so many kids home that I felt like I spent the bulk of my childhood mothering." At eight years old, I learned how to change a diaper, feed a baby, and burp them. My father worked long hours driving taxis and my mother spent a lot of time at the church and at her part-time job at Hudson's Department Store. Once I was old enough to be left alone at the house, I was put in charge of my siblings—and all of the foster kids that lived with us. "By the time I turned eighteen, I'd had enough. I moved out, struggled for a few years while working my way through community college." I shook my head as memories of that time filled my mind. "I don't know how I made it. I lived in some shitty places."

"And you never went back home?" he asked.

"Never. That didn't stop my siblings from wanting to move in with me. And I always felt like I had to let them, which was one of the reasons why I let Neil stay with me." It had been weeks, and I still hadn't heard from my cousin. Even though I was pissed—and would never deal with him again—I still prayed that he was okay, that he wasn't lying in a ditch somewhere.

"I understand. My siblings are all spread out." I was surprised to learn that Nero had siblings. He didn't talk about them much, and I knew it was because they weren't close, having been split apart when his mother died.

"Do you still talk to any of them?" I asked.

"Only my sister Sasha. She's down in Atlanta, though."

My phone buzzed with a reminder for my two o'clock meeting. I turned in his arms, searched his eyes. "I have to go." I kissed him. "I should probably make myself presentable for this Zoom call."

He fisted my curls in his palm, holding me to him. Then, he kissed me fully. It was all tongue and teeth, as his free hand roamed my body. Seconds later, my shirt was hanging off my shoulders and his mouth was on my breast, sucking my nipple until I cried out. His eyes flashed to mine, and he placed a finger over his mouth, signaling that I needed to be quiet. "I think I have the time to give you what you want," he murmured.

Oh damn, this man. My body sparked to life as he peeled my skirt off. His knuckles brushed my core, and I opened for him wantonly, not even caring that once again he had me in an extremely compromising position at work. He strummed my clit with his thumb before he sucked it into his mouth, bringing me to a quick, yet satisfying climax. Soon, we were making love, eyes locked, foreheads touching. It didn't take long for me to come again, shuddering around him as he pounded into me until he fell over himself.

Suddenly, I wanted more—more skin-to-skin contact, more time to talk. *More him.* "I think we should both take the rest of the afternoon off," I suggested.

His eyes flashed to mine, and a sexy half-smirk, half-smile formed on his lips. "You already know I'm down."

"Heffa, where the hell have you been?" Britt burst into my house, walking straight through my living room to my bedroom, peeking in doors along the way. She had on her standard work attire of blue jeans, a T-shirt, and gym shoes.

"Girl, why are you barging in here like the police?" I laughed to myself as my friend executed an imaginary search warrant. "What if I had company?"

Britt made her way back to the front door, where I'd remained. She folded her arms over her chest and tapped her foot against the floor. Narrowing her eyes, she asked, "Who is he?"

I shrugged. "What are you talking about?"

"You been fucking somebody," she said, motioning to my hair and my robe. "It's the middle of the day and you're home."

"As you can see, I'm home alone." Luckily, Nero had left hours ago for an early shift at the hospital. Because I still wasn't sure I was ready to tell anyone about us, last night was the first time he'd spent the night at my house. Up until then, I'd been going to his place. Partly, because I still wasn't comfortable in my home. Mostly, because I knew that people tended to just drop by unannounced. Things between us had graduated from sex during the day to all-night love making and mornings together. It felt natural. *And also very fast.*

Britt scanned the room again, presumably looking for clues. "I still don't believe it." She leaned in, sniffing my shoulder. "You've been very quiet. And absent for weeks.

I've been worried about you, but you don't seem to even care that you still have no furniture."

Ignoring my bestie, I walked into the kitchen and pulled out a carton of orange juice. I poured two glasses and let out a heavy sigh. "I plan to go shopping soon." I'd already purchased some things—a bed, a bedroom set, a television, and a new kitchen table—but I'd yet to find furniture for the other rooms. I figured as long as I had somewhere to eat and sleep, I would be good until I found what I wanted. "Besides, I work more than I'm here anyway."

Britt sipped her juice, eyeing me over the rim of the glass. "Did you go to your parents over the weekend?"

"Yeah." Every Saturday, I spent the morning and afternoon with my parents. During that time, I cleaned their house, took them grocery shopping, and ensured their prescriptions were filled and separated into their pill cases. They looked forward to that time together, and I never missed a week unless I was out of town.

Britt and I chatted about our families. I shared the latest on my siblings and even a little tea about Jada and her husband. Apparently, there was a little dust up at the church and Jada's husband was now on probation, on the verge of losing his job as assistant pastor due to some persistent rumors of inappropriate behavior with several female parishioners.

My best friend gaped as I told her the story. "Get out," she said. "That's what she gets being so judgmental." Jada couldn't stand Britt, probably because Jada's husband couldn't stop staring at my bestie's ass whenever she was in the room. "I told you he wasn't right."

"Girl, I know," I agreed.

Britt twirled her glass in her palms. "James asked about you again."

I rolled my eyes. "I told him when I saw him that it's not going to happen."

"He said he had stopped by the other day, but you weren't home."

While I was with Nero, I received the notification that someone was at my house. And that turned into a conversation about my ex. What's funny? I'd never been so open with another man about my life. Nero was easy. It was refreshing being around a grown-ass, sexy-ass man with no drama. When we weren't together, we sent little messages to each other or even chatted on the phone during our work breaks. He was a busy man, always on the go, always working, but he'd been intentional about spending time with me. It didn't matter what I wanted to do. He was down for whatever. I liked that. *I like him.*

"Any news on Neil?" Britt asked, pulling me from my thoughts.

The mere mention of my cousin twisted my stomach in knots. "Not a word. I asked Mama about him, and she hasn't heard from him either."

At this point, there wasn't much I could do about Neil. The police had taken the report, the judge had issued the warrant, but my cousin was in the wind. No telling when he would emerge, and by then, my things would be long gone.

Britt reached out and squeezed my palm. "I'm sorry, sis."

"I don't care about the stuff. It was never really about that." I angrily wiped away the tear that had burst free. "I'm just hurt that he did that to me, angry that he took Kitty. And mad at myself for trusting him."

"You can't blame yourself. You did nothing but help him." She walked around the island and wrapped her arms around me, resting her head on my shoulder. "Daphne, just continue being the person you are. God will handle Neil."

I shot her a sidelong glance. "Did you seriously just say that?" Britt was the last person to talk about God handling anyone. Not that she didn't believe. She simply hated so-called church speak.

Britt cracked up. "It's true, though." She cleared her throat. "Now, enough about Neil, who is the man you've been dissing me for?"

I should've known she would circle back to this. I hesitated to share, but in the end, decided that I needed her ear. "I did a thing," I confessed.

She lifted a questioning brow. "A thing? Or a dick?"

I swatted her with a dish towel. "Shut up."

"Well …"

"Both," I admitted. I motioned toward my new kitchen table, and we took a seat. "Remember I sent that text to Dr. Bond?"

"Right, and you were going to have a drink with him to talk about it. That was weeks ago." Her mouth fell open as realization dawned. "You're fucking him?"

I bit down on my lip. "Every chance I get."

Britt gave me a high-five. "Lawd, Jesus. You got dicked down by the good doctor."

I spilled everything, starting with the first date, and ending with us christening my new bed last night.

"Shit." She rubbed her forehead. "You like him, huh?"

"I more than like him."

"So this is serious?"

"I don't know." Admittedly, we hadn't talked about committing to each other. We'd just been taking it day-by-day, enjoying our time together. "He's so good, Britt. I feel safe with him. I don't even mind cuddling at night."

"Yeah," she murmured, "you're invested. Especially, if you're letting him spoon you while you sleep."

"Right? The hot flashes are real, sis."

"Girl, I know. I had one at the grocery store last night. I just walked over to the freezer section, opened the door where the Eggos were, and stood there until it subsided."

Leaning forward, I said, "I'm a little scared to move this thing out of the shadows and into the light."

"Why?"

"Because it feels too perfect right now in our little bubble. I want it to stay that way. Once the women at work know about us, the treachery will start."

"Well, you know how it is." She shrugged. "But you can't let that stop you. Have you met his daughters?"

I shook my head. "Not yet. But I did talk to his grandfather on the phone the other day."

"Does he know you're not trying to be someone's mother?"

"Of course. That's not an issue. He's done raising kids himself."

Britt searched my eyes. "I'm assuming you told me all of this because you need some advice, correct?"

"Not really. But if you had some words of wisdom, I might listen."

Britt had married young and lost her husband to gun violence. We raised their son together, and now my godson was a well-adjusted adult with a good-paying job and a baby on the way. I trusted her with my life, and I knew she wouldn't tell me anything but the truth.

"Enjoy him, sis."

Frowning, I asked, "That's it?"

"If you're looking for me to give you a reason why you shouldn't be with him, I can't do that."

I could always count on my friend to point out the

reasons why I shouldn't do a thing. Especially when it came to men. She'd even warned me about her own brother. So I was looking for more of that, like maybe she spotted a few red flags when I told her everything about Nero. But … no. "What about—"

"Stop," she chided. "Don't do that. Don't look for reasons not to be with him. We're not getting any younger. We're less than ten years out from the start of our third quarter in life. From everything you told me, this man seems like a keeper." She clasped her hands together. "For years, I've watched you put everyone else first. Why don't you try to just live your life? For you."

Britt had stunned me silent with this conversation. I stared at my friend but couldn't even think of a response.

She put me out of my misery when she said, "And if I meet him and he gives me a bad vibe, I'll let you know."

"Finally, something I wanted to hear."

"I'm not here to tell you what you want to hear, sis," she said frankly. "I'm here to tell you the truth. I expect the same from you always. So stop hiding him. Hold that man's hand in front of them thirsty, stiff women at your job and keep it moving. And bring him to the work site soon. I want to meet him, and we could use an extra hand."

We spent the rest of the morning together, shopping for furniture and talking about everything. My best friend had given me some great advice and I planned to take it. I just hoped it didn't come back to bite me in the ass.

CHAPTER 5
You Really Got a Hold on Me

DAPHNE

There was something about Nero. The way he walked, the way he talked, the way he … *Lawd.* I shivered as I recalled how he woke me up this morning, with his head between my thighs and his eyes locked on mine.

I wasn't an overly affectionate person. Never had been. Yet, when he was in the room, I found myself wanting to show and receive affection from him. I wanted to lose myself in his scent, in his arms, in his eyes. I just wanted him. At the same time, I couldn't deny that I was scared. Scared to love again.

I'd been in a few long-term relationships, had even walked down the aisle once—only to turn my ass around and run out of the church before I made the biggest mistake of my life. It was amazing Britt had run out with me, especially since the groom was her brother. James had scarred me, and since then, I'd kept myself at a safe distance from men. Good sex was one thing, but dick didn't pay the bills. Or keep me safe. *And sometimes it's available to every chick in the hood.*

Snapping myself out of those thoughts, I eyed the new furniture that had been delivered today. Britt was right. It felt good to get back on track, to try to move on from the Neil drama. Word on the street was that he'd moved to California. As far as I was concerned, he'd better stay there. Because I knew I wouldn't be able to stop myself from kicking his ass if he ever stepped foot in the "D" again.

Unfortunately, Kitty was never coming back. I missed that damn cat too. So much I'd spent the morning looking online for another feline companion. Still, even searching for a new pet felt wrong and made me resent Neil even more.

When my phone buzzed, I thanked God for my bestie. She always showed up on time, whether it was barging into the house or calling me at the exact time I needed to focus on something else other than my life.

"Hey," I said, fluffing my new throw pillows.

"Girl, you'll never believe what happened at work today."

"Tell me, chile." I'd spent many nights listening to Britt tell stories about her place of employment. From wives vandalizing their cheating husbands' cars to employees getting caught fucking on the line, there was a steady stream of tea spilled by my bestie. I knew way too much about the lives of her co-workers. *And I'm here for it.* "I need to hear about the latest assembly line drama."

I lit a candle and made my way back to the kitchen as Britt told me about the fight that broke out on the line several minutes ago. Apparently, one of the supervisors had two side chicks and both ended up on the same shift. Drama ensued when the women put two-and-two together, but instead of beating each other down, they'd attacked the supervisor.

Britt cracked up. "Check your messages. I recorded part of it."

I glanced at my screen and opened the video. The footage was clear as day. The man was on the ground and the two women were stomping the shit out of him. "Wait a minute. Why didn't anyone stop it?"

"Girl," Britt smacked her lips, "ain't nobody got time to jump into that shit."

"How did it end?"

"Another supervisor broke it up. But get this … his wife called one of the side chicks and threatened her life."

"He's married?" I exclaimed.

"For thirty years."

"He must have that magic dick."

"I heard it was average. One of my homegirls took him for a spin a couple of years ago. She said he couldn't even keep it hard."

Shaking my head, I offered, "maybe he's just really nice."

"He's an asshole," she grumbled. "But since he's nice looking and gives cash gifts, the ladies stay fighting over him."

Opening the fridge, I pulled out the pizza dough I'd prepared a few hours ago. Nero had asked me out to dinner, but I suggested we eat in. I loved being with him, but I was still hesitant to go public. And although he rolled with it, I could tell he was disappointed about tonight.

"Are you seeing your doctor tonight?" Britt asked.

"Yeah, he's on his way. I'm cooking dinner for him."

"You're cooking?" She snickered. "I can't get you to fry a pork chop."

"I know you lyin'," I tossed back. "I know how to cook."

Britt laughed. "Yes, but you don't do it much anymore."

My best friend was right again. When I was younger, I cooked most of the meals for my family. Once I moved out, I made it a point to cook only when I wanted to. "Well, today, I want to make dinner for my …" I hesitated at the word "man" because I wasn't sure I could really call Nero that. We'd yet to define our relationship and I was actually good with that.

"Your man?" Britt said, finishing my thought.

"I can't call him that yet," I admitted. "We're just hanging out."

"Hanging out and fucking," she mused. "Eating dinner and spending the night. It's been over a month. Hell, almost two. Sounds like your man to me."

"You get on my damn nerves," I muttered, grabbing the pizza sauce and the toppings from the fridge. I set everything on the counter. "I have to go."

"Don't hang up now, sis. It's crazy that you have a man, and I haven't met him yet."

A soft knock saved me from the lecture my friend was about to give me. "He's here," I chirped. "I'll call you later."

"We're definitely talking about this later," she warned.

"Bye, sis. Love you."

I ended the call, straightened my clothes, and hurried to the door. Swinging it open, I beamed up at my … Nero. "Hey!" I gave him a hug and a kiss, then pulled him into the house.

"Hey, baby." He pulled me back to him when I turned

to go back into the kitchen, capturing my mouth with his again. "You look good."

A smile tugged at my lips. I'd never smiled so much around any of the men I'd been with. Not only was he funny, but I actually felt happy around him. *Is he my man, though?* "Thank you," I murmured against his lips. "You look good yourself."

Whether Nero was wearing scrubs, a hoodie and jeans, or nothing at all, he was always fine as hell. It was an everyday thing. And I wanted *this* to be an everyday routine —greetings with kisses, talking about our workday, dinner, and *after* dinner. *He's probably my man.*

I led him to the kitchen. "I figured we could eat pizza and watch a movie."

Nero leaned against the counter. "How about we eat pizza and *make* a movie?"

I gaped at him, even as I imagined the movie we would make together. We talked about recording ourselves the other day. Before I could've never imagined it, but now … *I can't wait to watch us on camera.*

"Better yet," he continued, "you can eat pizza while I eat you."

This man—*my* man—could definitely get it tonight. *And every night.* I tried to keep a straight face, but my mind had already raced to the foregone conclusion that he'd be inside me in a matter of minutes. "What if you eat pizza and I wrap my mouth around your dick?"

He looked me up and down, igniting a fire deep inside that only seemed to burn hotter and brighter when he was near. Without warning, he hooked a finger in the waistband of my lounge pants, pulling me closer to him. He tugged my shirt off, then my bra. "I say we," he kissed my mouth, then ran his tongue down my neck and over my collarbone, before sinking his teeth into my shoulder, "save the pizza for later? You'll need to eat after I'm done with you." He picked me up in a fireman's carry—to my delight—and carried me over to my new couch. "Nice furniture." Nero set me on the sofa and pulled my lounge pants down. "But I'm down for all of the above."

Several orgasms later, we finally sat down to eat dinner. In my bed. Naked.

Nero bit into a slice of pizza. "This is good, baby. You made the dough yourself?"

I nodded. "I learned how to do it when I was a teenager. I was looking for dinner ideas and figured it was cheaper to make pizza than buy it. Since then, I've perfected the recipe."

He hummed his approval as he finished his first slice. "Tastes almost as good as you." He waggled his eyebrows, then barked out a laugh.

Giggling, I shoved him playfully. "You're so corny."

"That *was* pretty bad," he agreed.

I love it, though.

We ate in comfortable silence for a few minutes. "Are you all set for the Juneteenth Jubilee?" Nero had been engrossed in preparations for the health fair, so we hadn't spent as much time together over the past week.

"I think so. I'm sure something will pop up, but I'm ready to tackle anything that comes."

"I love that you're doing this for the community. I told my parents to put it in their church announcements. My dad was so happy when I told him I'd met someone from the Mr. Black Organization."

My father couldn't stop talking about the organization and its mission once I'd told him about Nero. Dad also spoke fondly about Ace and his brothers, too. He'd even pulled out some of his old pictures.

Nero chuckled. "That's cool."

"To see the spark in his eyes as he talked about good times with his brothas … It warmed my heart. I hate that he's lost touch with so many of his old friends."

My father rarely left the house anymore. Only to go to church and run a few short errands. It made me sad because he'd been such a busy person most of his life. I knew it had to be hard for him to take a step back, but his health had been getting worse in recent years, which made it difficult for him to move around like he used to.

"I'll have to bring him to one of the meetings with me. So that he can meet some of our new members."

"You'd do that?" We hadn't met each other's families yet—*And I'm okay with that*—but I loved that Nero had even offered.

"Of course." He wiped his hands with a napkin. "Do you have plans tomorrow?" he asked.

Frowning, I tried to picture my calendar in my head. "I don't think so."

"There's a barbecue."

I paused, pizza midair. Swallowing, I said, "Really?"

He eyed me curiously. "My cousin runs a barbershop. It's been in my family for decades. They put on an annual barbecue every June, to feed the community. I want you to come."

Averting my gaze, I blew out a slow breath. "Oh."

"Ace will be there."

Again, it wasn't the first time he'd asked me to meet his grandfather, but I still wasn't sure it was the right time. "Okay."

"What is it, Daphne?"

The fact that he'd called me by my first name instead of "baby" wasn't lost on me. I glanced up at him. "Huh?"

He sighed. "I've asked you to go out with me—in public—a few times and you've yet to say yes. What? Am I your dirty little secret?"

"It's not like that," I protested. "Not at all."

"Then tell me what it's like."

Running my thumb over the rim of my plate, I considered my words carefully. I closed my eyes. "I like being in our little bubble," I confessed. "I'm a private person. Once we 'go public'," I threw up air quotes, "people start talking. Rumors get started. I told you before, I'm not sure I'm ready for that."

"When *will* you be ready?"

I lifted a questioning brow. "Is there a time limit?"

He shook his head. "No. But I know what I want. I'm ready to be more than your private Bae. Is there something else holding you back? Your ex …"

"No," I blurted out. The topic of my ex-fiancé had come up in conversation a few times, but I hoped Nero didn't think I was holding back from *him* because of James. "My relationship with James is so dead I wouldn't even want to revive it. Most days, I can't even stand him. He's just part of my life because his sister is my best friend."

Nero stared at me. Correction … he stared *through* me. "I believe you."

I grabbed his plate and set it on the table next to bed. Then, I climbed on his lap. "I only want you."

"So, what's the problem?"

I'm the problem. "It's not you. It's me. I've spent my life putting everyone first. It's kind of scary to have someone who's willing to prioritize me. And … Fine. I'm scared."

"Of me?"

"Kind of. Of us. This wasn't supposed to be what it is.

I went to grab a drink with you and now we're spending nights together." I struggled to formulate my next thought but babbled on anyway. "I love it. But it's big, huh? What if it doesn't work out, and we brought our families into it? I've been there, had to send the thank you notes after the farce of a wedding. I'm hesitant to do it again."

He traced my jawline, placed a sweet kiss to my mouth. "We're very similar, you and me. You're smarter than me, though."

"How?"

"You didn't go through with the wedding. I married someone because I thought it was the right thing to do, and I was miserable. I wouldn't do that again. Getting to this point, feeling the way I feel for you … I'd be lyin' if I said it didn't scare the shit out of me, too. Yet, I'm willing to walk through fire to keep feeling this way."

My eyes fluttered closed as his words washed over me. "Nero," I rested my forehead against the side of his face. "You're killing me."

"I just want to make sure I'm not in this alone."

"You're not." I pressed my mouth to his. "I'm sorry if I ever made you feel that way."

"I get it. We're scared, but are we gon' do this?"

I searched his eyes, recognizing the sincerity in them. Because I felt the same way. Scared, but willing to walk this road with him. "I guess we're in this together."

He smirked. "So does that mean you'll show up tomorrow?"

Grinning, I twisted my body and straddled his lap. I lowered myself onto his growing erection and groaned when he thrust deeper inside me. "I'll be there."

CHAPTER 6

One Man Can Change the World

NERO

The barbershop was on ten as usual when I walked in. And the agenda was the same every day. Dissecting politics. Discussing the community. Talking shit. Ace was in his usual seat, near the back—away from the windows. I hadn't seen him in a minute, so I blocked off the entire day for him. It worked because I knew my family could use the help. The annual barbecue had only grown in popularity over the years, and people from all over the city had already started strolling in to enjoy the free meal.

The grill was going behind the old building and people were walking in and out. Families were spread out in the back yard, seated in lawn chairs, chatting with neighbors, and eating that good barbecue.

"Bottom line," Ace said, "many parents in the hood are raising a bunch of punks. Concerned more about social media than social skills. These lil niggas don't even know who the mayor of the city is. Never stepped foot inside of a voting precinct. Content to let their woman pay all the damn bills at the house. Can't tell me what they believe in. Don't even drive because they don't have a car." He shook his head. "Always riding around in their girlfriend's ride. Never their wife because they don't want to put a ring on it. And what the fuck is an Uber anyway? If shit goes down, how they gon' get up out of there?"

"That's it right there," my cousin, Ray, said. "I told my son to get his ass off my couch and learn how to do something other than playing damn video games and hanging on the block all day. He told me I wasn't respecting his boundaries. I kicked him out." He chuckled. "Then, my old lady snuck him back in while I was at work."

"Lost," Ace said, finishing his coffee. He tossed his empty cup into the trash and smiled at me. "My main man … where the hell have you been?"

I greeted Ray and the others, then hugged Ace before I sat in the empty chair next to him. "Working."

Ace grunted. "Maybe one day you'll play a little."

My great-uncle, Lou, agreed. "When I was your age, I worked, but I also had a lot of fun."

Growing up, I heard the tall tales about Ace and my uncles. To everyone around us, the Bond family was royalty. While I'd teased Daphne about believing the rumors, I knew there was more than a little bit of truth to them. My grandfather and his brothers had been revolutionaries in Detroit, men of distinction. They were known for getting shit done, speaking to the right people, and even kicking ass if needed. Even in his eighties, Ace had maintained a stellar reputation in the hood, and he commanded every room he entered.

Ace pounded fists with Uncle Lou. "That's right. I

remember piling in the basement, putting on a few records, and turning down the light. Y'all young fellas don't know shit about that."

Ray shook his head. "Why do we always have to talk about old shit? It's a new day."

Shaking his head, Ace said, "And you're teaching your kids to stay on your couch for the rest of their lives."

"Ace, man." Ray rubbed the side of his face. "Come on, now."

"I'm serious." Ace tapped his cane against the ground.

As healthy as Ace was, as active as he'd been, just knowing that he needed a cane hit me in the gut. Getting older wasn't for the weak at heart, especially for those left behind when the inevitable happened. Times like this, sitting in the barbershop on a Saturday, had become priceless. Because Ace and Uncle Lou were the last of the infamous Bond brothers.

Uncle Lou munched on some barbecue chips, pinning me with an intense stare. "When are you going to stop spending all that time at the office?" he asked, picking the conversation back up.

"I keep trying to tell him," Ace chimed in. "Money is good, but it's not everything."

"Right," Uncle Lou said. "And work won't keep your dick hard."

I cracked up. "Man, what?" I shook my head. "Don't worry about my dick, Uncle Lou. You need to be concerned about lowering your A1C levels."

Diabetes was prevalent in the Black community. Detroit had one of the highest rates in the United States. In my family, many were afflicted with the disease. Some had died. Not only had my mother succumbed to the disease, but my grandmother's fatal heart attack was a complication of Type II Diabetes. And Uncle Lou developed an eye disease after years of untreated illness and was legally blind. Watching them deal with this devastating condition, and knowing so many others who suffered daily, had propelled me to pursue a specialty in endocrinology.

Ray pointed at Uncle Lou. "I told you, Gramps. You need to stop eating all that fatty meat. Going to Mr. Corned Beef twice a week."

"Don't tell me what to do," Uncle Lou ordered. "Worry about that woman you call a wife and this fine establishment I started. Maybe invest in some updated chairs or something. This one is hard as a rock."

"You bought it," Ray said.

Uncle Lou grumbled a curse. "Twenty years ago, boy."

We all laughed. After cutting hair and dispensing wisdom for over fifty years, Uncle Lou had been forced to retire due to his vision loss. Ray had recently taken over and had worked hard to attract younger clientele. Which seemed to be working somewhat. But the OGs had this place on lock every Saturday.

Uncle Lou's wife brought him a plate of ribs. He bent down, a frown on his face. "This is not a rib, baby."

Ray snorted. "You can't even see, Gramps. You don't know if it's a rib or a *Mc*Rib."

Once again, the fellas erupted with uncontrollable laughter at Uncle Lou's expense.

Ace stood, motioning for me to walk outside with him. Once we hit the sidewalk, he asked, "What's the word?"

Confused, I glanced at him. "What do you mean?"

"Evelyn contacted me the other day looking for you."

"Shit," I muttered. "She's been calling every day, multiple times a day about the house." I accepted an offer on the house last month. The closing date was fast approaching, and she'd harassed me every damn day about it. "Now, she wants money from the sale."

"She wanted me to make you call her." He barked out a laugh. "I told her to talk to her mama and stop calling me."

I chuckled. "I bet she took that well."

I had no doubt Ace said exactly those words, too. He was brutally honest, had often made grown men cry, and didn't give a fuck what anyone thought about it. But it was those qualities that garnered him the respect he'd always commanded on the streets. Anyone who came to him for advice, money, or a place to sleep knew that he would always keep it real.

For years, I worked hard to distance myself from the trauma that had always been just beneath the surface. Losing both of my parents at such a young age could've destroyed me. Instead, being with Ace and Granny had saved me. After Mama died, the social workers were intent on putting me in foster care. He'd fought with everything he had, called in favors to some very influential people, to get full custody of me. I was grateful because I could've turned out differently.

On my first night with them, Ace sat me down and told me the rules of his house. There were only three—respect them, respect the struggle, and most importantly, respect myself. He also promised to never lie to me. He never coddled me, never forced me to do anything I wasn't comfortable with, and never made me feel like less than a man. At twelve, he took me with him to places I wouldn't have dreamed of entering at that age and dared anyone to say something. I learned how to speak to people, how to walk in a room and shut shit down, how to wear a Kangol, how to fight with words, and how to treat a woman. Living with him, watching him had changed me in profound ways.

"How's your friend, Daphne?" he asked. The two of

them had hit it off, even though they'd yet to sit in the same room with each other.

"She's good."

"I hope so. You've been in hiding since you started talking to her."

"I like looking at her," I told him. He'd said the same thing about Granny to me a long time ago.

He pointed a finger at me. "That's a good sign."

Glancing at my watch, I said, "She said she would stop by today, to finally meet you."

Ace paused, turning to me. "I want you and Daphne to go on a double date with me."

I frowned. "You're dating someone?"

My grandparents had married young, and he stayed faithful to her until her dying breath. After Granny died, he told me that he would remain single until the "Good Lord called him home."

Ace grinned. "I met someone, yes. We met at Eastern Market—during Flower Day last month."

Vendors from all over the Midwest visited the local market, selling everything from produce to jewelry to meat. The area housed local cafés and restaurants. Visitors could enjoy live music at Bert's Warehouse Theater, learn to cook, and shop for art among other activities. The venue held festivals and other events designed to bring people together from all walks of life.

Flower Day was a tradition for Ace and Granny, at least since the eighties. Granny had called it Date Day. They would disappear early in the morning and come back late with plants and different types of flowers for their house as well as other homes in their Rosedale Park neighborhood. It was their thing, spending quiet time with each other in the yard, digging up dirt, planting, and listening to old school R&B and smooth jazz.

When Ace told me he planned to attend Flower Day this year, I was happy he'd decided to return to the place that had made them so happy. What I didn't expect was for him to come back talking about another woman. At the same time, I was pleasantly surprised because I wanted him to enjoy the rest of his life.

Ace rubbed his salt-and-pepper beard, adjusted his Kangol, and waved a dismissive hand. "Nah, I still don't know if I want to go through all the rigmarole of getting to know someone else. I loved your grandmother. Plain and simple. Any woman would be a distant second to her." He clasped my shoulder. "If there's one thing I want for you, it's for you to find that same type of love. 'Cause Evelyn damn sure wasn't it for you."

I cracked up. "I already know that."

Ace sighed, and I noticed the sadness in his eyes. I wasn't so busy that I hadn't realized the date. It was the death anniversary of my father, his only son. After Dad died, Ace didn't really talk about him. Every time I'd asked a question, he would shut down. But I could tell it still affected him.

"Son, I blamed myself for so long," he confessed.

"For Dad?"

He nodded. "I thought I was too busy, too focused on the community to see that he was struggling." Shaking his head, he added, "I questioned my role as his father."

"You can't make someone be a better person, Ace." My father was a troubled man. His problems hadn't started with crack cocaine, but they ended because he'd made his drug of choice the center of his world. "Dad was an adult. He made his own decisions for his life."

Ace patted my cheek. "When I look at you, though, I feel nothing but pride. And I'm thankful that I've been able to watch you grow into the man you are today."

I lowered my gaze, suddenly struck with overwhelming emotion at Ace's words. "I hope you're not sick or anything, Ace," I muttered, finally meeting his gaze again.

Laughing, Ace waved a dismissive hand. "Nah, but I've always taught you to say the things you need to say. And stand by your word."

"If I haven't told you, I appreciate the role you've played in *my* life. I wouldn't be here without you."

Ace led me to his car and tapped the door with his cane. "Grab that box out of there," he ordered.

I glanced in the backseat, immediately recognizing the box I retrieved back in February, at the meeting with the brothas. I picked it up and handed it to him, but he wouldn't take it.

Ace shook his head. "It's for you."

Confused, I opened the box and pulled out a silver flask and three matching shot glasses. "Nice."

"I purchased that for your father a long time ago. But he never wanted to be part of the Mr. Black Organization." My father was the only man in the family that had bucked the tradition. All of my uncles and cousins were active members of the organization and served on several committees. "I almost forgot about it ... until you mentioned going to our spot back in February. I should've given it to you on your twenty-first birthday, the day you became a member."

I brushed my thumb over the engraving. The inscription was simple, since Ace was a man of few words. *Live free.* "Thanks, Ace. Appreciate it."

"I figured it's time we take a few shots together, to honor those who passed before us. Maybe one day you'll give the set to Zoe or Nala."

Nodding, I told him, "Zoe would love this. Nala? Maybe if it was a pair of kickz."

"That young lady is going to do big things. Watch."

"I believe it."

Ace pointed at the box. "There's something else in there."

Once again, I peered into the box and pulled out a smaller one. I stared at Ace as I removed the cloth wrapper, revealing a ring. I recognized it from one of Ace's old pictures, the same one that hung in the hallway at the meeting place. I studied the black Tiger's Eye ring, noting the intricate carvings on the band.

Ace squeezed my shoulder. "Powerful meaning. Powerful man." Then, he turned and started back toward the barbershop. "Now, come and eat some food."

It was just like Ace to do something sentimental and then walk away with no conversation. But there wasn't much to say. The gesture, the gift spoke volumes. It meant everything to me.

As we neared the front door of the shop, Daphne pulled into the parking lot. Ace paused at the doorway. "Is that her?"

I nodded. "Yep."

He gave me a dap when she got out of the car, dressed in jeans and T-shirt. The sneakers she wore were colorful, but stylish, and her hair was pulled up into a high bun. "You did good, son. You'll be alright."

I chuckled as Daphne approached us, a bright smile on her lips. "Hey." She stepped up on the tips of her toes to kiss me. Then, she glanced at Ace and gave him a hug before I could introduce them. "I'm Daphne. So happy to meet you."

Ace grinned. "I heard you were scared of me."

Daphne gaped. "Um," she stammered, "I … back in the day. But not now."

"I'm just playin' with ya." He squeezed her hand.

"Come on in, fix a plate, and listen to all the shit talking. If you can last through today, you're good to go forever."

She gave him a mock salute. "I'm ready."

As Ace pulled her into the shop, introducing her to everyone, I watched her charm every single guy in there with her smile. Before I knew it, Uncle Lou was flirting with her. He even put his plate down to talk to her. Which was no small feat.

Auntie Liz gathered Daphne and took her to the back of the shop. She glanced back at me and mouthed, 'Help me!' before she disappeared. I stared at the door long after she exited the room.

An elbow to my gut snapped me out of my thoughts, and I turned to find Ace looking at me, an amused gleam in his dark eyes. "Yeah, it's official," he said. "You should probably lock that down as soon as possible."

I glanced at him out of the corner of my eye. "Definitely."

CHAPTER 7
Inner City Blues

DAPHNE

"Then, he stole the boy's bike, his shoes—"

"And his coat," Uncle Lou added, interrupting Ray's story.

The men in the barbershop laughed as they explained the story of a young, destructive Nero who'd enacted revenge on one of the neighborhood bullies who'd beat up his little cousin Nick.

Ray chuckled. "In fact, he took his Nintendo, too."

"What happened next?" I asked, squeezing Nero's hand.

Ace took up the tale from Ray. "I took him right down the street to their house and made him apologize. Then, I made him work for Old Man Richards at the corner store every day after school doing odd jobs."

"Odd jobs?" Nero snorted. "The man had me cleaning shit out of the toilets every damn night."

Pointing at him with his cane, Ace nodded. "That's what yo' lil ass get. I told you time and again, fight with your fists and walk away with your head held high. What if the boy's father pressed charges against you?"

Ace continued the story, explaining that he'd tried to teach all the young men in the neighborhood that there were consequences to even the smallest actions. I didn't know Ace, but I suspected he was the reason the bully's father *didn't* call the police on Nero.

Uncle Lou chewed on a rib bone and nodded his head. "We lost some money on that little stunt you pulled, nephew," he confirmed. "I wanted to beat yo' hardheaded ass."

"What did you do to convince the man not to press charges?" I asked Ace.

He winked. "I'm old because I don't tell my secrets, Daphne."

Leaning in, I whispered, "I promise I won't tell."

Ace chuckled softly. "Maybe one day. Nero told me Henry Childs was your father."

I took a sip of my sweet tea. "Yes. I told him I was going to meet you today and he wanted me to give you a fist bump."

Ace reached out and bumped his fist with mine. "Ol' Hen … We had some good times. He used to drive for us back in the day. Cool cat."

I listened as Ace told me about the day my father helped him stay out of jail through his excellent driving skills. A protest at City Hall had gone wrong and the police were dispatched to break it up and arrest Ace and some of the organization's top leaders. I was transfixed during the story and couldn't wait to ask Dad about it. "Wow! I had no idea my father was that big a deal. I've only known him to be Deacon Childs."

"Yeah," Ace rubbed his beard, "he saved a few of us that day."

"Oh, yeah," Ray interrupted. "Wait 'til I tell you about the time Nero *did* get arrested."

Shocked, I looked at Nero. "You got arrested for real?"

Ray's attention was on the haircut he was currently giving, but he answered, "He sure did."

"Man, shut up," Nero warned. "You weren't there anyway."

"I know what happened, though," Ray argued. "I heard the story."

Nero tossed a clean towel at his cousin. "You talk too much."

"The lady needs to know what—"

A commotion outside drew our attention to the door where a disheveled male was standing. The men in the room stood up, Ray's hand reaching for his waist where I assumed he kept his gun. My eyes widened as Nero lifted his shirt, revealing his firearm.

"What are you doing?" I whisper-yelled.

Nero ignored me, his eyes focused on the man at the door. I tilted my head, trying to figure out where I knew the man from. The bright sun distorted his face so I couldn't make him out. Realization dawned on me just as the man stepped further in the place. But before I could say anything, he collapsed onto the floor.

Jumping into action, Nero ran over to him and checked his pulse while Ace made the call to 9-1-1. While Nero examined the semi-conscious man, he alternated between barking orders at Ray and asking the man pointed questions.

My stomach twisted in knots as I neared them, my heart beating hard in my chest. I was vaguely aware of the flurry of activity around me, but I couldn't focus on anything but the man on the ground. "Oh no," I whispered as I took in his face. A face that had once been so handsome, a face beat up by circumstance and time, a face I'd seen up close multiple times.

Nero glanced up at me, frowning. "Daphne?" he called softly.

"Is he going to be okay?" My voice was small to my own ears, but all I could think about was … *How am I going to tell Mom?*

Surprisingly, the paramedics arrived in record time. *Thank God.* But Nero didn't move. He continued to work on him, and even hopped in the ambulance, leaving me with Ace and the others.

Ace wrapped his arm around me. "I'm glad my grandson was here. It's a shame to see the young man like this. I remember when he used to walk around with those drumsticks all the time. So talented."

Another tear streaked down my face, and I rushed to wipe it away, but Ace saw it.

He squeezed my shoulder. "Daphne, are you okay?"

"I'm fine," I lied.

Ace glanced at me out of the corner of his eye. "Do you know Walter?"

"Yeah. He lived with us." I met his waiting gaze. "My parents fostered him for a short time."

After helping everyone clean up at the barbershop, I took food to my parents' house. While I was there, I told them about what had occurred with Walter earlier. Judging by his appearance, his efforts to stay clean had been futile. The last time I'd seen him, he looked healthy. He seemed so hopeful, so ready to get his life together.

While my mother didn't take the news well, my father had remained stoic. After sitting with them for an hour, I headed home. I busied myself cleaning and washing clothes, but eventually fell asleep on the couch.

The buzz of my phone woke me up. I glanced at the screen, answering when I saw Nero's name. "Hi." I sat up and stretched. "Where are you?"

"I'm outside."

I hurried to the door, swinging it open. "Hey," I breathed.

He cupped my face, pulling me to him and kissing me softly. "Sorry it took so long. I had to make a stop."

For the first time, I noticed a weird-looking box on the ground outside. I poked my head out of the door. "Was that there when you got here?" I asked.

He picked the box up. "I brought it with me."

I studied it, noting the big holes in the cardboard. "What is this?" I asked. From inside the box, I heard a tiny meow. My eyes widened and I lifted the top of the box. "Oh my God," I gasped, lifting the white and grey kitten out. "You bought me a cat?"

"A friend of mine knew someone whose cat had just had a litter. I made a few calls, and the owner finally contacted me when I was at the hospital. I had to drive to Ann Arbor to get it."

With tears in my eyes, I cuddled the kitten, grinning when it snuggled into me. "So cute."

"*She's* adorable," he said. "I immediately thought of you when I saw the picture."

My heart swelled in my chest. "Nero, I can't believe you did this."

"I know you miss Kitty. And even though it's not her, I feel like you'll grow to love this baby girl too." Nero brought in more stuff while I played with my new kitten—

wet and dry food, bowls, a litter box, bedding, and a toy. He shut the door and locked it. "That's it."

I grabbed the catnip mouse. "I think you went overboard on the supplies."

He shrugged. "I wasn't sure what to buy, so I just got everything I thought you might need tonight. We'll go shopping for her tomorrow."

For the next half an hour, we got the newest member of my household situated. "I think I want to name her *Coco*," I announced, dragging my fingers through her fur.

Nero frowned. "That's a weird name for a white kitten."

"Not really. Her soul is Coco."

He barked out a laugh. "I like it then."

I opened a bottle of wine and poured two glasses. He picked up Coco and met me by the sofa. We settled down, entwined with each other. "This is nice." I burrowed into his chest, while Coco stretched out near my foot. Craning my neck, I kissed his chin.

He brushed his lips over my brow. "I love seeing you happy."

The room descended into silence, and I wondered what Nero was thinking. "How is …?" He'd stayed connected with me via short, concise texts as they traveled to the hospital and even once they arrived at the emergency room.

"He's doing much better," he replied. "It's a good thing he walked into the barbershop when he did. How do you know Walt?"

I blinked. "Huh?"

"When we were in the ambulance, he called your name."

"He did?"

"Yeah. I thought back to how you reacted when you saw him. It's obvious you two have a connection."

"We do," I admitted. "He was my foster brother for a time. Even after he moved back home, he kept in touch with my parents. And me. I haven't seen him in a while. It was heartbreaking to see him in that condition."

"Ah, okay. Did you know he was an addict?"

"He's been using for a while. We tried to help him, but he relapsed several times. How do *you* know him?"

Nero brushed his finger down my arm lazily. "He lived in our neighborhood. His grandmother was one of our neighbors."

"Small world." I took a sip of wine. "I know you can't tell me what's wrong with him, but is he dying?"

"Not if he takes care of himself," Nero said. "I gave him my card again and told him to come see me. I hope he does."

"I heard you back at the shop." I recalled something Nero murmured to himself earlier. Something about insulin. "How did you know he was diabetic?"

"I saw him back in April and he had some of the signs then," he explained. "Today, he looked like he'd lost at least ten pounds since I'd seen him. Of course, I could've been wrong, but ..."

"You weren't wrong. Walter was diagnosed when he lived with us. No matter what my parents did to support him, he always had trouble managing his condition."

"Unfortunately, he's not the only one."

"He's alive because you were there."

"I'm alive because of *him*," he confessed.

Frowning, I turned to face him. "What do you mean?" I set my glass on the end table. "How did Walter save your life?"

"You heard the story at the barbershop. I was troubled." He chuckled. "It was worse before my mother died. I loved her, but she didn't exactly hold us accountable. She was always too busy with her next boyfriend."

I tried to imagine Nero as a child. Knowing him now, I couldn't picture him getting in trouble. He was so accomplished, so poised, so confident. "That must have sucked."

"I didn't know any better. My father had left her after I was born. She got with this asshole and had three more kids, back-to-back. Then, he left her. She did her best to take care of us. But she died because she didn't take care of herself."

I brushed my finger over his cheek. "I'm sorry you had to go through that."

He sighed heavily. "I was an angry kid, pissed off at the world. I started hanging with the older kids in the hood, doing shit I shouldn't be doing. One day, we decided we were going to rob the corner store."

"Seriously?"

"Yeah. We took two guns from my homeboy's house and walked to the store. Walt just happened to be on the block that day. He was in and out of his grandmother's house, as you probably know."

"Right."

"When he saw us, he stopped my ass from going with them. I still remember what he told me that day."

"What did he say?"

"Told me I was smart, had a good head on my shoulders, and that I needed to leave them fools where they were. I was too young to understand, but then he threatened to tell Ace." He smiled. "And I wasn't trying to get in trouble."

"So Ace was around when you were with your mom?"

"Oh yeah. He would come over to check on me. Let everyone around see him walking the street so they'd know he was my grandfather. I didn't appreciate it at the time because I wanted to do what I wanted to do."

"I'm glad he was there for you."

"Yeah. Anyway, I ended up going home that day. My friends followed through with the plan. One of them got killed by the store owner. The other two were arrested and sent to a detention center. They were never the same. Neither was I. After that, I started paying attention in school, spending more time on homework. I still fucked up every now and then."

"Right. You stole some kid's shit and sold it."

Chuckling, he mumbled, "Ray talks too much. But I graduated from high school with honors and received a full scholarship to U of M. I always said things could've turned out very different for me had Walt not been there."

I wrapped my arms around him, hugging him. "Walter said the *right* thing at the *right* time. And you made the *right* decision. " I kissed his shoulder, then his neck, and finally his mouth. "I'm glad you're the man you are now."

"Because you wouldn't have wanted my bad ass."

I tapped my chin. "Actually, Young Daphne probably would've been infatuated with you."

"Oh," he stood, cradling me in his arms. "So you have a dangerous side?"

I cracked up. "A little one."

He kissed me. "You think Coco would mind if I stole you for a few hours?"

I glanced down at my sleeping kitten, then back at the man who'd given me the best gift I'd ever received. "I think Coco is going to be knocked out for a while."

"Good. Because I need a shower. And I plan to fuck you against the wet tile."

CHAPTER 8
Signed, Sealed, Delivered (I'm Yours)

NERO

The Juneteenth Jubilee Detroit Event kicked off with the health fair on the Friday before the holiday. Every volunteer was present and accounted for, and willing to serve the community with grace. While the various organizations had held smaller Juneteenth celebrations for years, the decision to combine forces to put on an entire weekend of events had transformed the holiday for many in the city. With a different theme each year, local partners were able to cater to the diverse needs of our community. There was something for everyone—tailgate parties, a huge barbecue, speakers, a 5k walk, a literacy event. And now a health fair.

Watching everyone come together for a common cause was worth all the struggle to put this event on. I arrived early in the morning with Zoe and Nala. They'd been instrumental in helping me plan the health fair, and I couldn't be prouder of them. Everyone who'd helped put this event together had come through.

As I visited the various tents, I introduced myself to those who didn't know me and was met with smiling eyes and willing hearts. It felt good. At the entrance to the fair, we set up registration tables for those who wished to be seen by a health professional. So far, we'd had seventy people sign up for screening. Currently, the line was wrapped around the courtyard.

Food trucks serving healthy foods were stationed along the edges of the perimeter. Near the stage, people were watching a cooking demonstration. There were several vendors scattered in the area, offering everything from smoking cessation program information to guided meditations and yoga to on-site chair massages. The American Heart Association was on hand, along with other organizations, the local twenty-four-hour gym, and even the Wayne County health department.

Zoe ordered me to grab breakfast a few hours ago and had recently sent me off on a smoothie mission before I started my shift in the screening tent. When I arrived back, I handed smoothies out to my team, then sat down and got ready to work.

I'd screened at least twenty people before my phone buzzed.

Daphne: *It's too hot out there.*

Last night, Daphne had come up with every excuse not to wear her hair down today. She'd lost the rematch during our axe-throwing date, and I got to choose what I wanted from her. Smiling to myself, I recalled the expression on her face when I told her I wanted her to wear her hair down for an entire week. She'd scrunched up her nose and begged me to relent. She argued that the humid Michigan weather would make her hair swell up. She also explained the need for protective styles during summer months to mitigate damage to her hair follicles and texture. But I didn't budge. *Yet.* Tomorrow I would probably give in, but *today* … She was going to wear her curls wild and free.

"Why are you smiling, Dad?" Zoe asked, peering at me curiously. "You've been doing it all morning. Especially when you look at your phone."

I glanced at Zoe, before responding to Daphne's text: *See you in a few. If I see a ponytail holder, I'll have to spank you.*

Daphne: *You suck.*

Daphne: *And you can spank me anyway.*

I chuckled but decided not to respond to that. Glancing at Zoe, I asked, "Did you ever hear from Dr. Sanders?"

"Don't change the subject, Dad." Zoe wrapped her arm around my shoulder. "Nala and I have noticed that you seem a lot less tense lately. We want to know what's up."

Nala chose that moment to join the conversation. "Exactly."

I frowned. "Where did you come from? Aren't you supposed to be managing the children's activities?"

My youngest daughter had chosen to go into pediatric occupational therapy. She enjoyed working with little ones and figured that was where she would be needed. "I'm on a break. Shoot, it's hot."

"Enough about that," Zoe said, "who are you texting?"

Given my rocky start in life, there was no doubt in my mind that God was looking out for me when he placed key people in my path. Ace and Granny, Zoe and Nala, and now Daphne, had made my life so much sweeter. I rubbed Nala's hair. "I met someone."

Zoe's eyes lit up. "Really?"

"It's about time," Nala said. "I thought Mom had ruined you for everyone."

I barked out a laugh. "Really?"

Zoe shrugged a shoulder. "I did too."

Meeting Zoe's concerned gaze, then Nala's, I admitted, "Me too."

"Who is she?" they both asked at the same time.

Nala giggled, shoving Zoe playfully. "Better question," she tapped her chin, "is she nice. Not just nice to everyone else, but to you?"

"What does she do for a living?" Zoe tag teamed.

"And does she have kids?" Nala continued. "Her own house? Her own money?"

Pleasantly surprised, I listened as they interrogated me about Daphne. Their questions were thoughtful, and I could tell they were worried about me more than anything. I considered joking that I wished they were around when I met Evelyn, but I refrained. Once they finished round-one of their rapid-fire questions, I replied, "No kids. Owns a beautiful, newer home in a quiet neighborhood. Works at the university as a facilities director and never asks me for money."

By the time I finished responding to everything my daughters had asked, I spotted Daphne strolling along the sidewalk, with Lanelle and someone I didn't recognize. Our eyes met, and she beamed and gestured toward her hair. And I ...

Damn, I want her. Not just for sex, not just for play, but for the rest of our lives. She pointed at the tent and walked over to us, followed closely by her homegirls.

"Hey," she said.

"Hey, baby."

One of my medical assistants stopped what she was doing and stared openly at us. The way people talked, that one term of endearment would no doubt make it to the dean before the end of the day. Daphne noticed, too, because she raised a brow at the nosy assistant.

"Hey, girl," she said with a wave. "You might want to

pay attention to that blood pressure cuff. Don't want to cut the nice gentleman's circulation off."

While the medical assistant stammered a greeting before returning her attention to her patient, Zoe stepped forward, mumbling, "I like her already." She held out her hand. "I'm Zoe."

Daphne smiled. "Hi!" She gave Zoe a hug. "I've heard so much about you. Congrats on graduating from medical school."

"Hi, Daphne," Nala said, interrupting. "I'm Baby Girl."

Daphne greeted her the same way, with a tight hug. "Hey, Nala. So good to finally meet you in person."

Nala grumbled under her breath, "By the way, I'm glad you told ol' girl over there what's up. I almost told her off for staring at Dad like he was a perfectly cooked ribeye."

"Thanks for looking out," Daphne quipped, giving my daughter a high-five.

As Daphne talked to my girls, I greeted Lanelle with a hug.

Lanelle quirked a brow. "Okay, Dr. Bond. I see you!"

"Be quiet," Daphne warned, stepping over to us.

Ignoring her, Lanelle glanced at me. "Just sayin'. If you had to call someone *baby*, I'm glad it was my sis."

Daphne shook her head. "You're a mess." Then, she introduced me to her best friend, Britt.

I shook her hand. "Nice to finally meet you." In the time I'd known Daphne, she'd mentioned her friend often.

Britt smirked. "You too, Doctor. 'Bout time."

I wrapped my arm around Daphne's waist, pulling her closer. When she didn't try to pull away, I took it a step further, and bent down to press my lips against hers. "You followed instructions," I murmured, twisting a strand of her hair around my finger. "I might let you off the hook tomorrow."

"You better," she said, "because I'm not spending another afternoon out in this heat with all this hair down."

It was the first time we'd shown each other affection on campus, but I knew I didn't want to go back into hiding. "*Live free.*" Ace's words came back to me as we chatted about her plans for the day with her friends. In that moment, I realized the weight of those two words. Despite the past, the mistakes, the bad times, it was important to strive for freedom. Freedom from oppression. Freedom from bondage. Freedom to live the life I wanted. Freedom to love unconditionally.

Our relationship was still new. Both of us had been dealt with devastating blows, situations that should have rocked our foundations. Both of us had chosen to rise above our circumstances to carve out a good life for ourselves. It felt good to be with someone who understood me without words, someone perceptive enough to know my moods, someone who thought I was funny, someone who didn't judge me for my past, someone who didn't plan my future. I couldn't say I was in love yet. But I knew that I was falling. And I wasn't scared. If anything, I was ready.

After Lanelle and Britt ventured off toward one of the food trucks and my daughters walked away to meet their friends, Daphne sat in the chair next to me and held out her arm. "I think you should screen me."

"Dr. Bond?"

Daphne and I turned toward the entrance to the tent. She stood. "Walter? You're here." She hugged him. "I'm so happy to see you."

"Good to see you, too. It's been a long time." Walt glanced at me and grinned. "I went to the barbershop," he explained. "Ray told me you would be here today."

"Glad you stopped by." I motioned for him to take a seat. His drastic change in appearance was a good sign. He was freshly shaven, wore clean clothes, and new shoes. The scar on his face looked like it was healing finally.

"Nah, I'll stand. Can't stay long." Walt pointed back at a woman, who was watching us intently. "That's my wife, Selena." He waved her over to us.

When she entered the tent, I shook her hand.

She grinned. "Hi Dr. Bond. Thank you for your quick action at the shop. The incident was a wakeup call for Walt —and me."

I swallowed past the hard lump that had formed in my throat. "You're welcome."

"I wanted to talk to you," Walt said. "To thank you for saving my life."

"We have to look out for each other."

"Always," he agreed. "I decided to check myself into an inpatient rehab, in Wellspring."

"That's good. Sometimes you need to go away to get better."

"Right." He scratched the back of his head. "I plan to do my best."

"That's all you can do," Daphne interjected. "I'm praying for you."

Walt smiled at her. "Thanks, Daph." He motioned between us. "You and Nero, huh?"

She wrapped her arms around my waist. "Yeah, me and Nero," she confirmed.

He nodded. "He's a good guy."

"I know," she said.

"Well, we're going to head out." He grabbed his wife's hand. "Selena wants to grab a smoothie before we make the drive to Wellspring."

"Try the one with the pineapple, mango, and kale," Daphne suggested.

"We will." He hugged her, then gave me a dap. "I'll make an appointment to see you once I get back."

"I'll be here," I promised.

We said our goodbyes and watched them walk away. I plopped down on a chair. "That was something else."

Daphne rubbed my brow. "Something good."

I wasn't expecting the visit but seeing Walt hopeful and ready to at least try had given *me* hope. Pulling Daphne onto my lap, I rested my head on her shoulder, allowing her to hold me. "Things like this make me feel like I'm doing something right."

"Of course, you are, Dr. Bond. Look around you. People are responding to this event, willingly coming outside to get screened, to learn about living healthier lives. This is huge. You should feel proud of yourself and your organization for making this happen."

I peered at her and kissed her chin. "You're so beautiful."

She gaped at me. "I just hyped you up, Nero. Instead of trying to warm me up, you need to be taking blood pressures and pricking fingers."

Chuckling, I brushed my hand over her thigh and squeezed it. "I've been doing this a long time. I can multitask."

"Okay." She slid onto the chair next to me and held out her arm again. "Do your job."

Smirking, I wrapped my cuff around her, brushing my knuckles over her skin. As the cuff inflated, I held her gaze. While the machine worked to measure her blood pressure, I opened an A1C test kit. Once the machine finished, I scribbled the reading on the card we'd given to all participants. Next, I picked up her hand, lightly moving my thumb over her fingers. "Ready?" I asked.

Daphne stared at me through hooded lids and nodded. "Whenever you are."

Using a pointed lancet, I pricked her finger to obtain a blood sample. I inserted the test trip inside the digital monitor. While we waited for the results, I traced invisible circles over her arm. She was soft everywhere. I loved it. "My daughters like you."

She leaned closer. "I like them, too."

"Britt is cool."

"That's sis," she said with a shrug. "I love her to death."

"Are you good with today?"

Daphne stared down at my fingers on her skin. "If you keep doing that, I might need you to take a break and meet me in one of our offices."

I laughed, fighting the urge to pull her even closer. "You already know I'm down for that."

"You always are," she said. "Britt wanted me to ask you to pull up at her work site next weekend. She's renovating a home on the west side. She could use the extra hand."

Meeting her waiting gaze, I nodded. "Sounds like something I could do."

She sucked in a deep breath. "To answer your question, I'm definitely good with today."

"Are you hungry?" I whispered, keeping my voice low, even.

"A little bit. Are you?"

My eyes dropped to her mouth, then lower. I was hungry, alright. But I had a taste for something particular, *someone* particular. "I think I forgot something in my office. Walk with me?"

Daphne's eyes blazed with desire, affection, and something else I couldn't name. "What about my test?"

I glanced at the monitor just as the number flashed. "You're good. Below five percent. Normal."

She stood. "Then, let's go."

We practically sprinted to my office. Once we were inside, I yanked her to me and kissed her. I wanted to possess her, wanted to climb inside of her and never leave. I gripped her chin in my hand as I dipped my tongue into her mouth, playing with hers until she purred with delight. My heart pounded in my chest as we raced to remove clothing, never breaking contact with our mouths or our hands. Lifting her in my arms, I pinned her against the wall and pushed myself deep inside of her. I didn't even care if someone walked past my door and heard the commotion. We made love fast and hard, and when she climaxed, I did too.

Daphne slumped against me. "You've definitely spoiled me, Dr. Bond."

I kissed her again. "I want to keep doing it indefinitely."

Her eyes widened. "Are you serious?"

"You already know the answer to that."

"You don't say things you don't mean," she said.

"Right. What do you think?"

She brushed her mouth against mine. "I think … I'm down for whatever."

We made love again, taking our time as we found our rhythm with each other. She fell over first, and I followed her, with my mouth fused to hers as she shuddered beneath me.

Daphne giggled, motioning to her hair. "I told you my hair wouldn't make it today."

I glanced up at her and laughed, running my fingers through it. "Let's find you a ponytail holder, then."

As we spent the rest of the day together, working in tandem to ensure the event was a success, I was reminded that good could come from bad. While losing my parents was devastating, their deaths had allowed me the chance to learn from Ace, to thrive, to change my life. And while Daphne's cousin had hurt her to her core, I couldn't help but be grateful that she was so angry that she didn't pay attention to the text she'd sent. Because her cousin's betrayal worked for my benefit. Now, I was ready to begin a new chapter with the woman who made me rethink everything, the woman I wanted to go home to at night, the woman I wanted to *live free* with for the rest of my life.

Epilogue

AIN'T NO MOUNTAIN HIGH ENOUGH

NERO

Two Months Later

"I swear this game is rigged." Daphne tossed her axe toward the wood frame, groaning when it bounced off the wall and onto the ground. "Ugh! I suck today."

The sweltering August heat made it difficult to work, so when she suggested we forgo the outdoor concert at the Aretha Franklin Amphitheatre for air conditioning and another rematch, I agreed. "When are you going to give up and admit defeat?"

She winked. "Never. I'll go to my grave not admitting shit."

I barked out a laugh. "You're silly for that."

Daphne sauntered toward me, wrapped an arm

around my neck, and kissed me. "I will, however, concede tonight. Your place or mine?"

Summer was almost over, the semester would be starting soon, and Daphne had still yet to answer the question I'd asked two weeks ago. "Since you won't admit defeat, can you at least stop avoiding my question?"

Turning away, she charged toward the target and scooped up her axe. "It's a big decision, one that I'm not taking lightly."

I folded my arms over my chest and watched her miss the bullseye again. "Yes or no," I pressed. "Either way, I'm still here. We're still together."

Her shoulders fell on a sigh. "I want to say yes." She inched closer to me. "I really do."

"Say yes, then."

"But it's a huge step. And I'm used to living alone. I like my own space."

Tugging her forward, I rested my forehead against hers. "Same. And same."

"So why would we do this?"

"It makes sense to me. We're together every night. Why not consolidate?"

"Because you can always just go home when I'm irritated?" she offered with a shrug.

"Not." I pinched her nose, stood, and took aim at the target, winning the game easily.

"I can't believe you won again."

I gripped her chin and leaned in, nuzzling her nose. "This is just not your game."

Frowning, she stared at the floor. "If I move in with you, will you leave me alone when I say I need space? Or when I have a hot flash at night? Or when I—"

"Stop." I brushed a strand of hair from her face. She'd

worn it down tonight, which I appreciated. I'd show her how much later. "Yes or no."

"Do you know what this means?"

"Absolutely."

"Yes," she whispered.

I blinked, turning my ear to her. "Say that again. Louder for me because I'm pushing fifty."

"Yes," she repeated. "And you have four more years to fifty, baby."

Chuckling, I kissed her. "Was that so hard?"

Daphne grunted. "No."

"Okay, then. Your place or mine."

She lifted her arms up. "Mine, of course. I have a yard. You can barbecue and mow the lawn."

"I can *hire* someone to handle the grass," I corrected. "As far as grilling … I'll happily take over your grill."

"Fine." She nibbled on her bottom lip. "Nero, don't you think it's weird that we're moving in together before we even say the three words that most people say when they move in together?"

Daphne was everything to me. I realized I loved her right around the time she let me take her blood pressure at the Juneteenth health fair. The following day when she brought me breakfast in bed and let me eat my French toast on her stomach, it had cemented the notion. "What three words?" I teased. "Bend over, baby?"

The wicked gleam in her eyes told me that was exactly what she planned to do when we left. She confirmed it when she said, "Later."

"Make me come?" I asked.

She scanned the immediate area. Leaning in, she bit my ear lobe and murmured, "We'll definitely get to that later, too."

"I love you."

Her eyes flashed to mine. "Finally. I love you, too. Damn, it took you long enough."

I cracked up. "I told you that weeks ago."

Last month, we rented a vacation home in North Carolina. The agenda was simple—be naked as much as possible. And maybe a little sightseeing. We managed to go to the beach one day. The rest of the time, we stayed glued to each other. After we drank way too much wine, I serenaded her with Babyface songs. Right before I fell asleep, I told her how much she meant to me. Then, I told her I loved her, that I cared.

Daphne pulled back. "That does not count." She smacked my shoulder. "Those were lyrics to that song."

"But it was true," I argued.

"Say it again. Not in song."

"All jokes aside. I love you, Daphne. I love everything about you. I even love that you're a sore loser."

She shoved me playfully. "I can't stand you. There *is* such a thing as a sore winner, ya know?"

"I'll be that." I tugged the hem of her shirt, bringing her closer to me. "What I won't be is someone you can't count on, someone you don't trust. When I tell you I love you, I mean that shit."

Daphne rested her forehead on mine. "I love that you mean that shit. I love that I can trust it. I love you." Leaning forward, Daphne nipped my bottom lip. "Now, let's go home."

"Whatever you want, baby."

Subscribe to my Newsletter
New Releases, Upcoming projects, and Freebies!

In case you're interested, there is a Juneteenth Jubilee Freedom Weekend in Detroit! For more information, visit: juneteenthjubileedet.com

Baes of Juneteenth Series

Mr. Straight Up No Chaser by Sherelle Green

Mr. Right Now by Sheryl Lister

Mr. Down For Whatever by Elle Wright

Mr. Alpha Undone by Kelsey Green

Mr. Second Best by Angela Seals

Mr. Big Stuff by Aja

Mr. Play for Keeps by Kimmie Ferrell

Mr. Take Me As I Am by Iris Bolling

Mr. On Your Knees by A.C. Arthur

Mr. One and Only by Sharon C. Cooper

Mr. Tall, Dark & Unavailable by Tina Martin

Wait a Minute. Is that…?

Mr. Down for Whatever is a standalone novel with a surprising connection to a character I introduced in another series. Nero mentioned a sister. *Sasha.*

Sasha was a supporting character in my novel, THE WAY YOU HOLD ME. She also makes an appearance in IT'S NOT THEM, IT'S ONLY HER.

FYI… She will be back!

If you haven't already read my YOUNG IN LOVE Series, this is a good time to start.

It's Not Them, It's Only Her

My mission in life is simple. Family. Food. Freedom. Most people don't question my love for my family. And I make my living as a celebrity chef. The freedom part? The thought of being confined—behind bars, at a desk, or in a monogamous relationship—is not something I want for myself. Unfortunately, it becomes a problem when women want to make me their Forever Bae. Even after I make it clear that I'm not looking for more than short interlude.

Except... when I think of her, when I'm with her, I don't feel stuck. I actually want uninterrupted time with her. Surprised? Me too.

Want to know how I ended up in this predicament? I wish I knew because I definitely wasn't looking for it. Maybe it's the way she takes care of me? By listening to the things I say and everything I don't say.

Want to know why changing our relationship dynamic is a bad idea? I'm not the only one who wants her. Which makes it very complicated.

Want to know another reason why this is a bad idea? My track record speaks for itself. And she deserves someone good. I'm... not.

The choice is hers, though. I hate to lose so I'm playing to win. And I will show her that it's not him that she needs. It's me.

Excerpt: It's Not Them, It's Only Her

YOUNG IN LOVE, BOOK FOUR

The first hit didn't faze me. Because that muthafucka was weak. Always had been a punk. I was able to knock his ass out before his brothers joined the fight. I held my own for about ten minutes before I felt the blade slice into my side. Dropping to my knees, I placed pressure over the wound as another assailant knocked the wind out of me with a swift kick to my stomach. When I reached out to grab his ankle, I noticed my hands were covered with blood. My blood. *Shit.*

"Stay the hell away from my wife," the weak muthafucka spat from behind his brother.

I snickered, even as a sharp pain radiated down my leg. "Maybe if you knew how to take care of her, she wouldn't be trying to get in my bed." The right hook to my jaw caught me off guard, but it wasn't delivered by that asshole. Once again, one of his brothers had delivered a devastating blow. "The fact that you can't even fight me yourself tells me all I need to know."

I lunged for him, getting a few punches in before another brother—the one who looked like he spent his days lifting weights—slammed me onto the ground. In my attempt to shield my head from the hard cement, I landed on my hand, causing sharp pain to shoot from my finger to my elbow. *Shit, it's probably fractured.* I groaned, rolling over onto my back. And his big ass laughed. "You just don't learn, do you?" he taunted.

"Fuck you," I growled. "You better hope you kill me, because when I find yo' ass, when I'm not potentially bleeding out, I'm not coming to play."

His answer was a kick to my other side.

After taking several more severe hits, I couldn't find the strength to get up. As I struggled to catch my breath, I wondered if this was it for me. If the brutal beating and blood loss didn't kill me, dehydration and this damn Louisiana heat would. Them dusty-ass niggas probably thought the same because they scurried away like the pussies they were. I forced my eyes open but could only see out of one. The excruciating pain in my side had dulled to a small ache, but it still hurt to breathe. *Probably a broken rib.* Or several.

A moment later, I'd given up on driving myself to the hospital or even walking to my car. Luckily, I couldn't even feel the sweltering hard concrete beneath me anymore. My brief time in medical school made me acutely aware of my precarious situation. Dizziness. Shortness of breath. I was cold. And tired as hell. If I lost consciousness, I could die.

I managed to lift my arm, relieved that my Apple Watch wasn't damaged. Using all my energy, I asked Siri to dial the first name I could think.

She answered on the third ring. "What the hell is wrong with you? Calling this early in the morning."

Under normal circumstances, I would've told her she wasn't doing anything but sleeping anyway. Talking shit was my love language, but I especially loved the banter between *us*. But because I could barely get a word out, I simply muttered, "Come."

My arm fell under the weight of my injuries, and I promised myself I would fuck them muthafuckas up the next time I saw them. It took a damn stab wound and five big-ass niggas to knock me down. *But is this going to take me out?*

As the minutes ticked by, I found myself thinking of my family, of my parents, Always so giving, so understanding. They'd given us a blueprint to live by, taught us how to navigate the world while Black. They'd shown us unconditional love in action every day. Never made me choose between what *they* wanted and what *I* wanted. They'd only encouraged me to go after what made me happy.

My mother once told me to stop taking so many risks, to stop tempting fate. If she only knew the shit I'd done… Aside from this particular situation, I'd fucked up more times than I'd ever admit to her. What would she do if I died in the street alone over some bullshit? I chose to mess around with a married woman and now bore the brunt of her husband's anger. In my defense, she'd told me she was separated. I didn't believe her ass, though. I just didn't care. Maybe because I was young and cocky. More likely because she was fine as hell, and I was a man-whore. At least, according to my sisters and Skye.

In my weakened state, I sent up a silent prayer, going through the Lord's Prayer and asking for forgiveness and protection as my mom and Sister Pearl had taught me back in the day. All those years in Sunday School mattered. A moment after I sealed my prayer with an "Amen," I wondered if God even heard me. It wasn't like I'd spent so much time talking to Him. But I wanted to plead my case, though, to argue that my brothers and sisters needed me. Well, six of them needed me. Not Tristan. He didn't need shit, but I could imagine even he would be devastated if I was no longer here to blame for his shortcomings.

Who's going to tell everyone when they're fucking up? Paityn would blame herself, for not being there, for not giving me enough love and understanding. But she'd always been a person I could count on and the only person that might be able to beat me in the kitchen. *Maybe*. My baby sister, Blake, would probably go to jail or die trying to avenge my death. My chest tightened when I thought of Blake's twin sister, Bliss. All I could see is her sad face in my mind. Dex and Dallas… They called us "The Triples". Dex and I were identical twins and Dallas was our fraternal sister. She always thought that made her an outsider, but she was the best of us. Hell, they all were a hell of a lot better than me. And Asa? My baby brother would probably just leave. He was good at disappearing. Guess he got that from Tristan. Demi would probably be quiet. She wouldn't speak, she wouldn't cry, she wouldn't engage. It was her defense mechanism, but also her most comfortable state. And she would retreat to that space. X, Zara, Skye… They weren't just friends. They were as much my family as my siblings and parents.

Tears filled my eyes. I wanted all of them to be happy, to know how it felt to be in love, to be loved. I hoped someone would pick up a spatula and cook something besides Paityn. Maybe my niece, Raven? I needed my father to know how much I admired him, how he inspired me to be great. And I prayed my mother didn't blame herself for my mistakes.

As my eyes drifted closed, I whispered my love for them to the night air and imagined their faces in the stars. And then everything went black.

"Duke?"

A voice. *Her* voice pulled me back to the present.

"Please," she whispered, emotion in her voice. "Don't do this to me. Don't make me explain this to Dallas. And your parents? Oh God." I felt her forehead against the side of my face. "I'm sorry. I'm so sorry. I shouldn't have left you there. You were drunk, and I knew it wasn't a good idea."

I winced as a needle pierced my skin. Coolness replaced the sting and I realized someone had started an IV. Other sounds registered next. Male voices, spouting vitals. A hand wrapping a blood pressure cuff around my arm and another set of hands applying pressure on my side.

"Stay with me," she pleaded.

It's not your fault. I wanted to tell her this was on me, that she did nothing wrong, but the darkness pulled me back.

Sometime later, I awoke to unfamiliar voices around me, the sound of a blood pressure cuff deflating, and the consistent beep of the heart monitor. Opening my eyes, I scanned the area and realized I was in a hospital room. Two doctors were off to the side, discussing my care with a nurse while another nurse flushed my IV. And Demi was sitting in the chair next to my bed, her eyes on their movements.

"Not your fault," I managed to say finally.

She jerked back, meeting my good eye with a watery gaze. "Thank God." She stood and hugged me. Gingerly.

"I'm sorry," I whispered.

Demi peered up at the ceiling, before leveling her gaze on me again. "You scared the shit out of me. And you're right, it's not my fault. It's yours." Tears fell down her face. I wanted to wipe them away, but I still couldn't move. "I prayed."

"Me, too." I closed my eyes.

Demi flashed a wobbly smile. "You need to pray

harder, because you look like you've been walking through the valley of the shadow of death. Face all fucked up, eye looking like Rocky's after Apollo Creed won the match."

I would've tried to smile, but I knew it would hurt so I murmured, "You're silly."

"Adrian!" she called, mimicking Rocky in the movie.

"Stop," I chuckled. "You're killing me."

The doctors walked over to us and gave me the rundown of my injuries. They'd operated to stop the internal bleeding and started me on intravenous antibiotics to prevent infection. The good news was the knife didn't hit an artery and my ribs were bruised, not broken. *Just like my life.*

When they left the room, Demi brushed a finger over my brow. "Are you in a lot of pain?"

I shook my head. "Not right now. Did you call my family?"

She quirked an eyebrow. "Did you want me to?"

"No."

"That's what I thought." Her chin trembled. "You could've died."

"I didn't."

"But you *could've*," she reiterated. "I'm glad you didn't, though. Get some rest."

Acknowledgments

God is so good!

To my family and my *framily*, I love you all! Thanks for having my back.

To my lit sisters… OMG! I couldn't have done this without you! Thank you!

To Midnight… Once again, you saved the day! Thanks so much!

A special shout-out to the awesome readers , bloggers, and writers that I've met on this journey. Thanks for your support. I appreciate you!

Connect with Elle!

Subscribe to my Newsletter
New Releases, Upcoming projects, and Freebies!

On Facebook,
Join my cocktail lounge for exclusive updates, drink recipes, and lots of fun!
bit.ly/EllesCocktailLounge

Visit my website: www.ellewright.com

Email me at info@ellewright.com

Thank you for reading Dexter's story! I love to hear from my readers. If you enjoyed *It's Not the Hookup, It's the Chase*, please consider posting a review or sending an email. They really do help. Don't forget to tell your friends!

About the Author

There was never a time when Elle Wright wasn't about to start a book, wasn't already deep in a book—or had just finished one. She grew up believing in the importance of reading, and became a lover of all things romance when her mother gave her her first romance novel. She lives in Michigan.

Connect with Elle!
www.ellewright.com
info@ellewright.com

facebook.com/ElleWrightAuthor
twitter.com/LWrightAuthor
instagram.com/lwrightauthor
amazon.com/Elle-Wright/e/B00VMEWB78
bookbub.com/profile/elle-wright

Also by Elle Wright

CONTEMPORARY ROMANCE

Edge of Scandal Series

The Forbidden Man

His All Night

Her Kind of Man

All He Wants for Christmas

Once Upon a Series

Beyond Forever (Once Upon a Bridesmaid)

Beyond Ever After (Once Upon a Baby)

Finding Cooper (Once Upon a Funeral)

Jacksons of Ann Arbor

It's Always Been You

Wherever You Are

Because Of You

All For You

Wellspring Series

Touched By You

Enticed By You

Pleasured By You

Pure Talent Series

The Way You Tempt Me

The Way You Hold Me

The Way You Love Me

Distinguished Gentlemen Series

The Closing Bid

Women of Park Manor

Her Little Secret

Carnivale Chronicles

Irresistible Temptation

New Year Bae-Solutions

One More Drink

Young In Love Series

It's Not Me, It's You

It's Not Love, It's Business

It's Not the Hookup, It's the Chase

It's Not Them, It's Only Her

Baes of Christmas

Ten Christmas Shots

Smoke and Burn Series

Some Kind of Love

HISTORICAL ROMANCE

DECADES: A Journey of African American Romance

Made To Hold You (The 80s)

SUSPENSE/THRILLER

Basement Level 5: Never Scared

www.ingramcontent.com/pod-product-compliance
Lightning Source LLC
LaVergne TN
LVHW090527110826
845146LV00003B/1010

* 9 7 9 8 9 8 5 4 5 4 2 4 6 *